Poetpourri

A Labyrinth of Wandering Thought

by
Myron Ferdig

Published by Ferdigwerks
P.O. Box 176
Tujunga, CA 91043

www.ferdigwerks.com

Illustrations by John McNees -- Battle Creek, MI
nowillustration@gmail.com

Printed in United States of America

Poetpourri

A Labyrinth of Wandering Thought

Apologia

Ah, yes! Come into my scented labyrinth
Stocks, roses, hyacinth
My peculiar potpourri.....
Draw in color, sounds, aromas, visions
Let your mind wander
Ponder essayed witticisms
Indeed, you'll have your criticisms
Mingled together into a veritable
Sort of 'Poet-pourri' -- if you will

Yes, that's it!
A Poetpourri!
A Labyrinth!
A Maze!
A litany!
A fragrant or a pungent phrase!
Feel along the white-washed walls
Use your senses, draw from all,
Absorb the smells --Go ahead, Mon!
Take your time!
Feel all the feelings in your mind!
Wander on and on and on.....
No bread crumbs, torch or GPS,
A full day's jaunt would be my guess,
Unless of course, you run..... or rest --
Joy, pain, hope, despair,
Some fresh, some ancient, heavy air

Preface

I've dabbled in short stories since -- well I guess since grade school, ... but alas, now all "by the wayside," and I can't remember any storylines.

From about six years of age, I read everything I could get my hands on, including Edgar Rice Burroughs, Clarence Mulford, James Oliver Curwood, James Kjelgaard, Felix Salten, Roy Rockwood and Joseph Altshelter.

The first book --outside comic books -- of any substance I recall reading was over 400 pages, titled *Four Little Blossoms at Sunrise Creek* by Mabel Hawley... followed closely by *Bomba the Jungle Boy on Jaguar Island,* both written in language a six year old tyke could grasp. They held my interest beautifully; I was hooked on books!

By eight I had read just about everything on my sister's book shelves, from *Bambi* to *A Tree grows in Brooklyn...* and by ten, my name must have been scrawled on cards of most library card pockets at the local school and town library.

Only recently - since being retired - have I set apart some time to write... poetry, short stories, and songs. It allows (as a friend says) some creative juices to flow; it also gives satisfaction.

We all have choices.

I hope you choose to enjoy my offering.

Myron Ferdig
November 2015

Table of Contents

Table of Contents - cont.

Table of Contents - cont.

Book Seven - Took a Turn For The West!

Book Eight - At Last.....Sunlight!

for

DAR*l*ene

She Who Inspires Me

Book One

Into The LAbyrinth

Up Near Fredricksburg

The hist'ry books are filled with tales of
Guts and much bravado,
But blood and grit and sand and shit
Express it - just a shadow.
No one can feel exploding hearts,
Rubber limbs, useless parts;
No one can write the smells of fight,
The horror of the battle.
Or fear expressed when eyes assess a bloody,
Empty saddle.

It happened up near Fredricksburg,
We blue coats was a'nappin';
Before they came, twas eerie quiet –
With just a flag a'flappin.

Oh, on occasion nightbird sang,
Coyote yapped, skeeter stang...
Then someone shouted "Johnny Reb!
Comin up the river!"
And most like me grew skin like geese,
And pangs down in his liver.

Captain held a gloved hand up,
Midst cries all weak and giddy --
"Now keep a sharp eye, mind your nerves,
Weapons at the ready!"

I prayed there in the waning light,
Prayed for strength, prayed for might;
Sure, one can set a steely jaw,
Fix bay'net to his rifle,
But sure as hell his fleshy craw
Is jellied mor'n a trifle;

For who could tell this log of hell
And capture all it's color,
The senses of a man grow dull,
And by the minute, duller;
They get into a trancey mode,
Just shoot, reload; shoot, reload;

Nostrils fight the acrid smells of sweat,
And piss, black powder --
And through it all, your comrades fall --
And demon death screams louder!

Fellas' minds went mad that night,
Men from both sides scattered;
Most of us that made it through were bloodied,
Filthy, tattered...

My leg got mangled by a ball,
Below the knee, ... won't lose it all

Says Cap,"My lads, brave lads ye be,
But beaten by the Southern."
So, Captain held one gloved hand up,
White flag in the other'n.

Southern General Lee came riding in
To honor all the troops,
Spouted off some "cock-n-bull"
Amidst the Reb's war whoops...

Then Lee and Cap they both agreed,
All able hands to tend the need...
So, with the moon, and through the night
We tended dead and dyin;'
I wasn't much of any use,
But I determined trying.

Among that mangled heap of flesh,
I found a younger cousin;
He wore the grey of enemy,
Just three -- four mor'n a dozen.
I dragged myself up to his side,
Raised his head, and 'fore he died,
"Papa, would you pray for me?" he said,
And then was gone...

He could have been my kid, your kid,
For sure, some brother's spawn.

General Lee glanced o'er at me,
An' I think a bugle tooted;
I know for sure I held his gaze,
And sure we both saluted!

Now I sat there in the 'proaching dawn,
Reb on lap, one leg gone,
Pecular sight I must have been,
A man of forty seven --
My tears, his blood, were mingled,
as I cradled him to heav'n.

It happened up near Fredricksburg,
We blue coats was a nappin',
Before they came, twas eerie quiet –
With just a flag a'flappin...

(a work of fiction -- MEF -- July 2012)

6

<u>*Gramps*</u>

For fifty years I've plied my craft --
A craft reserved for men,
And yet, (and you may think I'm daft)
I'd do it all again.

I've seen craftsmen who've come and gone,
My grandpa among 'em...
But my grandpa ne'er steered me wrong,
All his life he 'couraged me on...
This tribute here's about 'im.

§ § § §

The old woodworker gave a nod
As in his store she sauntered;
"So what brings you into my shop?
Just what is it you wanted?"

"Grandpa you are such a tease;
I'm here to start my lessons."
She gave his arm a loving squeeze --
"And I have Father's blessing."

"You here to learn woodworking, Missy?"
"I ain't in no mood to teach some sissy!"
"Your Pa agreed? Must be some joke;"
"Saws and such are for menfolk!"

"You should be at the kitchen sink!"
But he gave a sidelong wink --
To her relief --
So, on tiptoes, and very brief,
The youngster up and kissed his cheek.

Her grandpa wrinkled up his nose,
Shook his head, brushed his clothes;
The old man sighed, said, "I suppose ....
"Did you bring all your gear?
"Your goggles, gloves, and steel-toed boots?"
Let's stay safe in here."

"Yes," she said, " "I truly did
It's here inside my pack;
And the fella down at the hardware store
Said I could bring it back!"

"Bring it back?" the craftsman cried,
"Did my son raise a quitter?"
"Not on your life!" she shot right back,
"I'm your new baby-sitter!"

They both enjoyed a hearty laugh
Then Grandpa cleared his throat --
And for the next one hour & half
He talked while she wrote:

"First off, I'm the captain of this ship,
You're the 'prentice' at my hip,
I'll teach you where and when to chop,
But if I say sweep the floors or mop
In this small woodworking shop
You must obey my rules."

"Yes sir, Grandpa, I surely will!"
But her grand dad -- he was talking, still....
"Now, fingers you can lose or save...
On band saw, planer, edger, lathe --
Be prudent, careful -- not a knave;
This is not a place for fools."

So the next few weeks right after school
Her gramps would teach about each tool,
He'd quiz her on her memory,
Try her on ability,
Give her either "A" or "B",
That was pretty cool!

Jobs would come into the shop
Her lessons changed, but never stopped,
Simply took on a different flavor;
And these were moments she would savor.

She watched intently as he worked --
Never cranky, never irked,
Traits she grew to emulate;
Grew up tall, grew up straight.

The day he said, "Make me four wheels."
Was a day she still remembers.
"8" round and 1" thick --
From those old walnut timbers."
She ran the wood through the planer,
To exactly 1" thick;
Then sliced it into 1 foot squares,
Yelled, "This should do the trick."

Though he pretended not to watch,
Her grand dad's eyes were glistening;
Under his breath he whispered praise
But his apprentice wasn't listening.

She built a jig and cut the rounds
Then sighed with satisfaction;
"You mumbled something? I heard sounds...
But I needed no distractions." "Just
so, just so," her grandpa said,
Looking so relieved;
"While you were on that scroll saw, child,
I don't think I breathed."

"Grandpa!" the young apprentice chirped,
"Time you take a breather!"
Then she poked him in his ribs,
"In truth, I didn't either."

§ § § §

And so, for, I guess, twenty years
They both worked the wood;
Building, fixing, making stuff --
And what they made was good.

She knew 'twas coming when grandpa said,
"My eyesight, child, 's no longer good,
And I don't earn my pay;

I'd best quit, girl, while I'm ahead,
Hang up my steel-toed boots I guess,
And just call it a day."

"But, you'll do just fine
In this shop of mine --
Girl, this shop is yours to keep --
Just let me sign on the dotted line...
While I can see,
And while the daylight lingers..."
Then grandpa gave the gal a squeeze...
"And I still have all my fingers."

I buried Gramps, fingers and all
I guess, some 3 years after --
We made his box of Cherry wood --
Both he and I together;
We made my box as well.....and good,
... Sits on a shelf to weather.

Gramps is gone where craftsmen go,
But gifts? He left me many...
His patience, wisdom, skill and wit
Now stand beside, and guide me.

April 2015

Old Grey Skirt

The old grey skirt was out once more,
Picking through the barrows;
I'd seen her many a time before,
Where the ancient Norbridge narrows.
A wearisome looking lass was she,
Maybe 80 odd.
"Better she than me," I thought,
And finished with, "Thank God."

Almost double bent, she was,
And ragged were her clothes;
"There ought to be a law," I thought,
As down the street she goes.
Big as brass, this tiny lass
Pushed a shopping cart --
"Stolen from a Ralph's or Von's," I mused,
"Or other nearby mart."

Full of bottles, cardboard, cans,
And other trash donations --
I surmised her daily haul
Would barely give her rations.

I decided then, upon a whim,
To shadow as she tottered;
And sat amazed, in SUV,
At the many blocks she covered.

I watched her as she passed folk by,
With friendly word or nod;
Then watched her disappear with buggy
Into the salvage shop.
"Ahhh , now," I mused, "she'll wander home,
To scrounge another day."
But, smiling out -with cash in hand,
She went a different way.

Her fingers nimble, deft and swift
As she searched among the rubble.
Amazing! How fast filled that cart,
Although she stooped halfdouble.
Such industry! Such Energy!
A Champion 'gainst defeat!
And of a sudden, this frail lady
Looked to fill the street!

And so, I spent the afternoon,
Watching in amazement,
As Old Grey skirt -- bright cart in hand --
Pounded down the pavement.
Three more times she gathered up --
And sold with satisfaction;
Did she do this every day?
Brain reeling in reaction --

Did she lose husband to the war?
Was she a flood survivor?
Did she lose all to bankruptcy,
With no means to revive her?
As told, I spent the afternoon,
Reflecting on her plight --
Her youth, her children, financial losses,
How she spent her nights --

My mind could scarcely take it in,
And I felt so ashamed;
I'd thought to merely have a laugh,
But my heart rearranged --
And as I pondered holding back
The tears that tried to flow,
This little thing in tattered grey,
Stood tapping at my window!

"I've seen that you've been following,
In that grandiose machine;
You tried to hide a time or two --
Hmph! as if you can't be seen.
My goodness! Just what is it, sir?
I Doubt rape would be your deed;
And if it's robbery, son, I swan,
You'll get but chicken feed!"

"Book, then, is it? You writing a book?"
The little lady queried --
"You couldn't do a book on me
Until I'm dead and buried!

Don't get your pencil out just yet,
I'm hungry, tired and cold;
You can drive me to the Burger King...
Oh, I know I'm being bold.

A very nice girl works in there,
I think her name is Clare,
I have a special booth to sit,
And she supplements my fare.
Clare knows as soon as I step in,
If I, or she must pay..."
I smiled, put cart in SUV,
Said, "I'll be Clare today."

So we sat there in a corner booth,
Across from one another --
To any casual passersby,
She could have been my mother.
She smiled a wispy little smile --
Said, "This is like a date."
I replied, taking both her hands in mine,
"Dear, this is more like fate."

Today I learned a lesson
Most valuable to me.
I've planned each facet of my life --
Just how it had to be.
My car gets washed on Tuesdays,
Fridays go to Al's;
Every Monday evening
I play poker with my pals.

Though I have everything I need
My life is quite a bore.
Today you taught me with your life
That less is sometimes more;
You walk as though you own the world
And labor hard and steady,

And yet with people that you meet,
Your smile is always ready."

Old Grey Skirt just smiled at me,
And said, "It's time to go.
You may begin with pencil, friend,
For now I'll not say no.

Just take me, if you'd be so kind, sir,
To the edge of town."
So that I did, both she and cart,
Then slowly drove back down.

Now, many an evening at my desk,
I write of things that haunt me -
Of Old Grey Skirt, her life, her loves,
Of things -- as she would want me.
And many a dawn I find myself
Where ancient Norbridge narrows --
And walk a bit with Old Grey Skirt,
The lady 'mongst the barrows.

Spring 2012

The Monster Frog

The big, green Kenworth sat
    under the elm
        Midst leaves of red and gold;
She was polished to a mirror shine
    Though 24 years old.

LeRoy bought her, spanking new
    Back in '87 --
Racked up 'most 2 million miles
    'Fore LeRoy went to heaven.

He named the rig the *Monster Frog*
Recorded the name in the Truckers' Log --
Emerald green, with golden trim,
Seems every truckstop knew of them.

In all those miles that LeRoy drove
    Little Sassy sat beside,
From their home in Citrus Grove
    Ridin' *"shotgun"* since a bride;

From Seattle down to Tallahassee
Every Roady's, Dixie, Flying J --
Truckers knew the "Sassy Lassie"
The *Monster Frog*, and of course, LeRoy.

The stories they could tell, those folks,
    Of Sassy's smile, of LeRoy's jokes

And on the road, no finer friend
If that big, green *Frog* came round the bend.

Why, even today, some old-timer
Will spin some tale in a truckers' diner
And light up the eyes of some young buck
'Bout LeRoy and his monster truck.

§ § § §

Now, every day at 5:30 sharp
Sassy walks to where the *Frog* is parked;
'Gainst the elm Miss Sassy leans
And peers up at that big green machine --

"LeRoy what'd you go and die on me for?"
She grabs the bar and climbs aboard.

(Now that truck ain't moved
In the last 6 years)
But, dreaming, fighting back the tears
The lady sits - eyes half closed
Ridin' *Shotgun* down some dusty road --

Then she adds that trip in her Trucker's Log
And hops back down from that *Monster Frog.*

12/21/2013

Early Lunch

We sat on the breakwater wall,
Eating an early lunch --
Tuna salad on toasted sourdough --
Couldn't eat it all --
Ate most of it, though....
Tossed the rest down below.
It was immediately attacked by a frenzy
Of squawking greed
Not nearly enough to satisfy that feathered need
...

To our left some 30 feet down the wall
on beach blankets of various color
lay topless young ladies, two or three
We knew just about where they'd always be
So we climbed the wall for the scenery --
The seabirds, sea, sunbather

At the tideline, some thirty feet in front of us
Sandpipers, plovers, terns, stilts and willets
Like Monday morning vacuum cleaners
Awkward, yellow-legged babblers
Veritable confederates --

All muttering and yammering together
As they scrounged among the salt spray pebbles
In their quest for savory delectables --

Watching these smaller waterfowl
I remembered boyhood, and how
with Pop and Mom we'd stroll along the beach --
Pop would take off shoes and socks
Roll his pant legs up
Mom would lift up her skirts
To keep the muddy, roiling surf
Just out of reach
As we searched the tide pools, disturbing rocks
Turning them over
Just like the sandpiper, stilt and plover ---
To find our treasures underneath.

My friend tossed a half-chewed apple core
Seagulls from everywhere, screamed for more!
Took one last look to my left for dessert
Dropped down from the wall --
Lunch was over --
Back to work.

Dec 2015

The Fishing Hole

To poke around my dreamy past
I'd sometimes reel Sometimes cast,
I'd find a grassy knoll to lie,
To drift among the cumuli
W' one leg swung o'er other knee
And gaze into eternity;
To catch those special times of mine...
Some vinegar, some hearty wine...
"A fine bouquet..." I'd hear me say,
And waken from sweet slumber.

The thoughts of carefree, childhood days
Were intertwined -- a crazy haze --
But, e're so often one popped out
And thrashed and splashed as would a trout:
The lady run o'er with my bike;
Catching 'crawlers' by flashlight;
Barging in, as sister bath'd --
She was twelve, an' I just laughed --
Building bonfires in the fields;
Tapping maples, cooking yields;
All these things -- they salved my mind...
And warmed me, altogether.

Aaah, there! See? The line goes taut!
A lovely memory I have caught:

"That's it! Keep his head up, lad!" ...
I'm ten, and fishing with my dad.
He bellows, dancing with delight,
"We'll have ourselves a feast tonight!"
He slips and slides and halfway falls,
And runs the creek in overalls,
But proudly holds my biggest catch,
Slips it in my gunny sack;
Big, wet arm slaps round my back,
And we laugh home to Mother...

Children, four -- three born at home,
Perfectly to teeth and bone,
Rebecca Lynn, she comes to mind,
Midwife nowhere -- way behind,
"I'm here, Hon. you're doing fine...
The head has crowned, I can't tell yet.
Has anybody got a net?"
We laughed, she pushed -- before Lamaze;
Oh, what a lovely thing she was,
Covered in this whitish grease;
Midwife knocks -- a hug -- relief!
With scissors!

Langenheim: now, there's a name!
Our doctor when Lorinda came.
She set her bag beside the bed--
"You *will not push* just yet!" she said.
But Ms doc L. seemed quite perturbed
Cause no one trembled at her word...
But there was an effort/face turned red...
And Lo! Another daughter!

--With a "You GO Girl,"... flashed a peace sign,
Singing, *Jeremiah was a Friend of Mine*

All sung in C ..4/4 time,
And "*Let it Be*" ..... ok...ok...ok!
OK, That <u>was</u> a whopper!

Jon, of course, before the gals
Was already my five year old pal
He came to me as part of a pact
Hell, I never woulda tossed him back
Definitely a keeper...

When he was just a little fellow
His favorite thing was riddles
He had some good ones...
Like "how do you shoot a blue elephant?"
But he always added..."No thinking!"
So we --that is --his ma and me
could never get them right...

One year we went to the Grand Canyon
Jon, he thought he'd have some fun
So right in front of everyone
He jumped over the edge.
Well, I must say we were all stunned
His mother thought she'd lost her son...and
She screamed and cried
Terrified! ... and .....
Well..... See,   there was this ledge.......

Elliott came last by seven years
Born at home like the other two
Something women "just should not do!"

Strange how most folks think today
There could be no other way
Besides a hospital:
"Why, we have stirrups, forceps
Amniotic hooks
And of course, a scalpel.
And the room we put you in is sterile."

Well, in spite of that, Elliott came out whole...
and he's almost normal.....
uhhhhh, well.....
Except for Metallica & AC/DC
"Turn that cassette down 1600 decibels, please!"

§ § § §

to continue...

Brutish thoughts come strolling in,
(I thought I'd put them in a bin) But,
there they sit, "You reeled us in!
Now, feast upon us, Brother!"
Snake pit! Anguish! Forever! Through!
"Love to dance, but not with you!"
Angeldemonfillyshrew
Embellishedwithascrewyoutoo!.......
And, panting, ploughing back to shore...
I'll jig that pond no more!...
§ § § §

Nothing Like A Day-Dreamy Afternoon- Fishing

So, I fast-forward into time
into this cloudy dream of mine
With...."Come on in! The water's fine!"
And we were skinny-dippin'!
.
See, we'd been fishing in this pond
But steelhead stayed where fish belong;
It was so hot...before too long
My Joy was in the water.
I joined her in our stream of play
We must have frolic'd hours away;
"You're all shriveled up!" I heard her say...
That's when the neighbors caught'er.

Knee deep, stares up -- wide-eyed --stands,
Don't know where to put her hands;
"You boys could act like gentlemen!"
They vanish in the trees.
Joy gets out, finds her bra,
"You recognize those fellows, Pa?"
Gales of laughter. "I sure do.
And Ma, I think they'll remember you!"
We end the day, laughing, with a brew.
.....So, in my creel, another.

§ § § §

So many memories I have had
Most are good, some are bad
Some to relish, some to salve
Of children growing into men

of daughters giving birth...and then
Of childrens' children
I'm getting old!
Must be -- getting bald, not quite so bold --
And pains becoming manifold!
This world of technicality --
It strains my mind! Can hardly see
My knoll of warm serenity!

My computer, do you realize,
Has a forty, a *forty* gig hard drive;
And it's a toy compared to others...
A changed world this..... compared to mother's!
Why, you can fish and fish and fish all day
And blow your mind -- and time, away!
But, <u>*is it useful*</u> knowledge -- that?
Sometimes, I'd rather have my cat....

Rebecca brought him home to me,
And Ralph, he wouldn't let you be!
I owned a shop, and Ralph was official *Greeter*...
A client would come, and Ralph would meet'er
Climb right up her boots and jeans,
Yawn and stretch until she'd see
That scratching his ears was the only means
Of getting through to me.

One morning before I went to work
I heard a squawk -- why this pint-sized jerk

Had caught a full grown, Mallard duck
And brought him quackin', flappin' in to me!

I dropped my jaw, laughed like heck,
"Hey Ralph! Let go this poor boy's neck!"
The duck, though mangled in the wreck
Was grateful to be free....
Ol' Ralph -- now there was one
who reeled in memories by the ton --

Life is filled with ebb and flow
It's sometimes stop and sometimes go
Sometimes yes, sometimes no
There are things to hide, things to show
I've always loved the life I've lived;
Searching for the positive.
To focus thoughts, to see, to feel --
To hold them close, to make them real
Then stuff them, oh, so gingerly,
in my aged creel.
To later call them back to mind
Sup on them, like vintage wine --
All those folk whose lives touched mine
As well, the lives that I have touched --
I pray I've not destroyed too much...

§ § § §

Ahh, the oranges, reds and yellow-browns
Autumn leaves coming down

Breeze is blowing them around
Time for me to hurry home

Grab creel, and reel and fishing pole
To my long forgotten grassy knoll
Back to my favorite fishing hole.

W' one leg swung o'er other knee
I'll gaze into eternity;
Once again, toss out my line .....
To jig among the cumuli
To catch another memorable time...
...hoping for a lunker.

Summer 2003

Prairie Grass

Like flaxen hair blowing horizontal
tufts here and there left untouched --
other -- swirling west, then north
at the mercy of the unseen cause --
providing an eerie, mesmerizing scene.

blades springing to new life,
having been beaten down
into roundish beds --
some singly, some in groupings
of threes and fours --
a sort of communal gathering
in the darkness.

The sights and sounds now
of small flocks of cowbirds
busily harvesting
on morning's sundrenched strands
of wooly shoulders,
while young ones
poke and pummel upward
seeking nourishment from grazing,
snorting, but otherwise
seemingly indifferent mothers.

chatter of small rodents
popping up, lecturing with voice of disapproval
on yesterday's invasion
of the massive intruders --
only to disappear once again
into nether regions,
scampering to another
dwelling entrance,
to pop up yet again with that same disapproving
vocality.

By early afternoon insistent bellowing
signals: 'time to move on' --

leaving behind those too ancient,
too feeble or too maimed to continue;
leaving behind jackals of the desert
to scavenge;
leaving behind the scores of scolding landowners;
leaving behind life-giving,
replenishing nourishment
for the newly-harvested
prairie grass.

Spring 2015

The D-47 Roadsters

An old Buick still sits in Franklin's field
On the knoll, neath that ancient
Weeping Willow;
Day before he went to war.
It was driven there by Molly's father, Leo.

They spread a blanket on the leather
'Neath a nightsky full of stars
And spent that last night there, together...
Molly, so she says, was conceived by Mars.

Leo never came home --
Left Molly and her mother all alone;
And though many tried to buy it --
Take that 1915 Buick from that tree,
Molly's mother would deny it;
She'd shoo them off and tell them, "Leave it be!"

We moved to that farm in '27,
So it's been there 'least ten years, maybe eleven.

Rag roof was torn and all caved in,
Rust was showin' on the tin,
And a crop of oats was growin' through the floor.

Leather seats - both front and back
At one time spoke of richness and of splendor;
But now horsehair peeps up through the cracks
As nature takes that Buick back --
Rain and sun, as one,
Bid her: Surrender.

§ § § §

We called ourselves the D-47 Roadsters --
Boasted six members in the club;
Called one another 'Cylinders' --
Jimmy, Joe, Molly, Harvey, me'n Dutch.
We had to let Molly in...
We only had five men,
And well, with one cylinder missin'
it wasn't somehow fittin';
'Sides, Molly was the only Franklin in the bunch.

We took turns behind that big ol' wooden wheel,
Jimmy could VRROOOM! -- Like an engine roar;
Almost sounded real.
We'd go up to Collier's General store...
(Collier's ain't there no more)
Anyway, none of it was real;
All make believe,
Just sittin' neath that tree.

Molly would point out the car window
As we whizzed along,
"Oh Look! There's a cow with a calf!"
So we'd all point, stare, look back and laugh.

Glass was all gone --
Busted out long ago --
One of our members, I suppose...
Coulda been me,
Or maybe Joe,
I don't know...
And no one cares
Or remembers.

You couldn't just join the D-47s --
Had to be at least seven,
And no older than eleven,
After that you were dismembered!
I turned twelve the next December...

You had to be invited
And answer questions I recited --
Of course, based on that old Buick in Franklin's
field --
Like: How many wheels had brakes?
How much gas the fuel tank takes?
How many Horsepower does this engine yield?

And I also remember
Initiation for new members:
Drag a bucket of soapy water up that hill,
Wash the Buick, sweep'er out,
Shine the headlamps and the grill.

§ § § §

Last Thursday afternoon I finished up the plow,
Shut my John Deere down and grabbed my
duffle;
Meandered up that hill,
Leaned against the willow,
Pulled out a blanket and a pillow;

Spread them there
o'er coils of springs
Showin' through the leather,
On top of which I lay a sprig of heather,
A bunch of roses,
Champagne, 2 glasses and a ring.

That night our love was sealed;
We were laughing , Molly squealed
In the back seat of that Buick D-47!
Then we lay there -- gazin' up to heaven.
We were 'tween seven an' eleven
Up, 'neath that willow in Leo Franklin's field.

§ § § §

Time and years have driven by
But we still wander up there and lie
In the back seat, 'neath that wondrous sky;
We hug, we laugh, we cry

As we grow together older....
Just two remaining cylinders
Of those Buick -Model D-47 Roadsters.

Oct 2015

The Sentinel

My home was once on the rugged slopes
of Hartley Bay.
You know the area --
just south of Kitima-at Village
and the more recent Kitimat township....

We, my kinfolk and I, stood as sentries,
oft'times shrouded in mists and low cloud
offering shelter to our many furry and feathered
companions, dealing out provender
to the smallest of God's species.

We thought we were old as dirt --
perhaps we were --
at least, as old as memory.
We were standing solemn and proud,
long before Cascadia
struck our whole coastline in 1700,
toppling and crushing
many of the "lessers" as we called them,
splitting, grinding, and destroying --
yet restructuring the topography --

On its heels the devastating high water
that came from the sea....
Such a drenching!
It reached almost, but not quite as
far up the ravines
to come within mere meters of where we stood..

Some of us simply shook off the event,
in remembrance of stories of the elders,
of a similar, far more devastating occurrence
which destroyed much of the lower coast --
listed by human historians as
the Neskowin event some 1800 years previous --
epicenter of which was actually many
hundreds of kilometers south;
I was not yet formed,
but in my soul,
I remember.

§ § § §

We heard them long before we saw them,
excavators, grapple yarders, skidders, chokers --
And the fellers with that awful,
horrifying sound of chain saws --

We watched as they devastated slope after slope,
coming ever nearer;
watched as our age-old relatives --
Scores of our own kin --

grandmothers, aunts, uncles, virgin daughters,
topple down hillsides,
to be plucked up and fall prey to the jaws
of soul-less beasts, dragged by cables
to the will of *"The Machine"*

And then, they were upon us -- Us,
who had stood here for centuries;
Us, who symbolized, signified, yea, even
sanctified safe haven --

Laughing and cursing they came,
churning up the hillside,
bellowing foul!
Destroying the stillness
of this pristine mountainside,
destroying the sanctuary of the cougar and bear
destroying the *Aerie* of the sea eagle,
who so proudly
feathered her nest almost 100 meters
above the ground
in my sheltering arms ...
I wept that day.

§ § § §

I and 67 of my fellows were part of
the initial slaughter;
We were felled, battered and bruised
and lay in heaps of threes and fours
strewn on top of each other,
then dragged singly to a limbing area
where a monstrous, smoke-belching set of teeth
devoured arms and greenery within minutes
spitting out chunks and bits
not suitable for it's appetite.

I was to be next victim
to those terrible chain saws;
to be ripped into
two lengths of 35 meters,
leaving one of 22 meters...
But a foreman decided instead,
that I was one of four so magnificent,
that I would be given special care,

and for that I was horse drawn, as were
my three fellows,
clumsily and painfully
all the way down that mountain
and into the sea -- ending in a roped-off area
they called a "log sort."

for the others, a fierce set of jaws
swooped in to hoist them,
each one, onto a waiting vehicle
with a ten foot wide wheel base,
and tires almost 3 meters high;

then most of those majestic specimens were
winched down
with three sets of steel chain,
each one biting into hide
with tremendous pressure.
They then rode down
a poorly constructed dirt and gravel
excuse for a roadway,
and upon arrival to this watery "log sort" --
were dumped, without ceremony
into the sea.

The vehicle then roared
back up the mountain road.
I was happy to have been, at least,
pulled by a horse.

§ § § §

All day long my fellows came,
to be herded - battered, bruised

behind the rope
by a "dozer boat" operated by a guy
called a "grader" or "sorter"
who selected us
according to his view of acceptance.
We knew what lay in store:

Those of a certain type were to be crammed
into container vessels and then shipped
to slaughterhouses
along the China/Russia border --
to be changed into 1" x 12s", plywood, fencing,
or perhaps, pulp paper!

Can you imagine?
My Canadian instincts
deplore such an idea!
Every fibre of my being
cries out against it.....
As yours ought!

§ § § §

Three of us escaped when a rush of
current and tide swept the dozer boat
sideways forcing its propeller against,
and cutting through the corral rope...
the tidal surge continued on,
pushing us out to sea
where current, fate and providence
issued a writ of freedom.
Currents
of the Queen Charlotte Sound
took us wherever they pleased --

passing in, around and in between
several small passageways in the Island group --
I never saw my fellow escapees again.

I ended up in Bella Bella,
where five fishermen - three men,
One teen aged girl and her 10 year old sister
waded into the icy water to pull me to shore.
My rescuers immediately
roped both my ends,
then went to tell the Fathers of their find.

Almost as quickly
I was swarmed upon
by a host of these *Heiltsuk* peoples
who, without exception, wept.
Wept that such a magnificent specimen as I
had met such violence!

Yet they seemed pleased that I had been put in
their hands
They had plans for me,
plans - not of destruction in some far off sawmill,
paper plant or plywood factory.

But the First Nations peoples
of the Village of Bella Bella --
the *Heiltsuk* --
had plans that would give me a portion
of the dignity I had had only yesterday:
Me, whose life had been dedicated to safety and
protection
The harboring of wildlife within and under my
branches

Their plans included
a large, tall and straight totem,
standing erect --
With bear cub scratching its back at my base,
With cougar scratching and sharpeneing her
claws on my barkskin
And high up, with eagles' outstretched wings,
once again providing at least symbolically,
a comforting and safe resting place.

A length of me would be given as an offering
to the neighboring Nuxalk peoples
from Bella Coula
for another magnificent totem;
There would be plenty for sea going canoes,
carvings and artwork by skilled First Nations
craftsmen and women
To whom I willingly share my heart.

§ § § §

I have been made part of an ocean going
canoe envoy -- going up and down
the north and south coast,
inviting First Nations peoples to partake
in a traditional Qatuwas tribal council --
a peoples' gathering
in Bella Bella.

Once again I stand tall and proud --
now at the entryway of two villages --
partaking of potlatch,
Offering symbolic protection and security
to all within my purview

I am the Sentinel.
I am at peace.

August 2015

Book two

Foolish On Every Side!

Please Wait for the Site Operator

Please wait for a site operator to respond.
You are now chatting with 'Tony'

Tony: And how may I help you, today?

Me: Hello Tony
I seem to have my computer lock up on me...
Intermittently.
And when I push the space bar, the whole
computer goes down.

Tony: Let me check that

....

.....

.....

.....

Me: Did I lose you Tony?

ME: HEEEEEELLLLLPPPPPPP!

...

...

Tony: Still checking on it;

Me: I had choppers and the coast guard on high alert

Tony: Thank you for waiting --

Tony: Is this a common occurrence?

Me: Only when I'm on line.

Tony: Are you being funny?

Me: Only intermittently.

Tony: So what can I do for you today?

Me: My computer locks up.

**Tony: Yes, Intermittently... I know.
But what can I do for you?**

Me: Where are you located Tony?

**Tony: India. The Best Computer Techs are in India.
Now.........,
What Can I do for You today?**

Me: How do you know that to be a fact?

Tony: I get paid big bucks. How can I help you
today?

Me: Right now, nothing. My computer seems to
be working fine ...   right now.

Tony: We regret any inconvenience this has
caused you; have a nice day.

*Please wait for a site operator to respond.
You are now chatting with 'Tina'*

Tina: And how may I assist you, today?

Me: Hello Tina, where is Tony?
He hung up on me.

Tina: No Tony here. You are speaking with
Tina.
How may I assist you?

Me: Where are you located, Tina?

Tina: In my office. How may I assist you this
evening?

Me: It's still morning here, Tina ....Where is
your office?

Tina: In North Korea. The best Computer
Techs are in North Korea.
How may I assist?

Me: Why do all you people think you have the
             best techs in the Universe?

Tina: Because it say so on our chat queue
             script. Universe?
Let me see..... ahhhh, no! no universe. World—
             really big!
         Now, how may I help you?

Me: I seem to have my computer lock up on
             me... Intermittently.
And when I push the space bar, the whole
             computer goes down.

Tina: Hmmm just the space bar huh? Does this
             happen every time?

        Me: Intermittently.
        And only when I'm on line.

Tina: Thank you for waiting. I'll be with you in
             just a moment.
                        ...
                        ...
                        ...
                        ...
        Me: Hello...Hello? Anyone There ?
                        ...
                        ...
Tina: Your Prepaid minutes of service expire
             after six months of inactivity.

Tina: While this has been part of our Terms of Service for years, we have just recently begun to enforce it.

Me: Wow! Did I lose you, Tina!

Tina: Hmmm, funny haha ok, push the space bar.

Me: OK.   --------See? It's fine right now, but....oh,oh there it go.......!

Tina: Hmmm, ok, Everything look good. Good! push the space bar agai----

Please wait for a site operator to respond. You are now chatting with 'Mark'

Mark: And how may I help you, today?

April 2014

Empty-Headed Suzy

"**S**uzy, you have one problem",
Said her older brother, Ed
"You're cute and everything, like that
But you've got an empty head."

"The teachers teach you stuff alright
And you understand the stuff you hear
But every time you tilt your head
That stuff falls out your ear."

"Not to worry, Suzy
Here is what we'll do, then
We'll create a brace
Stick it in place
From your shoulder to your chin"

So a brace Ed made for Suzy
From her shoulders to her chin
Then read a book aloud to her
To fill her head again

Suzy sat and listened
Her head was upright, straight
And being scientific
Ed said "Now we sit and wait."
"Does the brace feel comfortable?"
Is the shoulder strap too taut?"
Suzy laughed and ----

"Oooops", said Scientific Ed,
As Suzy shook her empty head,
"It's worse than I ever thought"

Stuff tumbled to the floor
With every shake that Suzy made
"We must think this through some more
The brace is out, I'm afraid,"

Suzy sat and cried, "Boo Hoo!"
And tears fell down like rain
"Don't cry Suzy, I'm telling you.
You'll get water on your brain!"

"I have a great solution!"
Said her scientific brother,
"We tried and failed the first attempt,
Let's try with another!"

Once again, Ed read a page
Again her head was filled
"Now, we'll put plugs in your ears and nose
So nothing will be spilled."

Minutes came and minutes went --
They enjoyed a conversation,
Then Suzy sneezed!–The plugs were sent -
In *ev-er-y* direction!
Complete with stuff! — Thundering Tarnation!

Empty-headed Suzy

Brother Ed gave up on her,
He runs a charity.
Packed up all his scientific stuff
And gave it all to me.

That was fifteen years ago
You ask what happened to Suzy?
She's married now—how do I know?
Oh, I've never been too choosy.

April 2014

The Grand Prize

Menfolk were the feature at the county fair --

Must of been 'least twenty of us there.

Idea was to get a week's cheap labor
  Mostly have some fun with single neighbors
  Get token paid as well, to do some favors.
  For the ladies

So here we were just standin' in a row - shirtless,
  if you please
Some skinny, some with bellies to our knees
"Without no shirt, ain't no one here I know,"
  Said the ladies.

Now after the week was bought
Back to the fairgrounds we'd be brought
Was it worthwhile or was it not
To the ladies

We'd be judged through the ladies eyes
Best worker'd get a great grand prize
Only one - there'd be no ties
No if's, or's ands, but's or maybe's
And no whining by the guys
Only ladies

So, Millie lambert started off the biddin'
"Ten dollars for old Henry Jacks" she cried,
Mary chuckled, "Mil, you must be kiddin'.

"No, I ain't. I'll have him paint inside."

"Paint? Can he paint? asked Rose O'Grady
"Then fifteen bucks for Ol' Henry", said that
lady
Millie got real huffy then at Rose
I thought for sure that they'd soon come to
blows.
Meantime while they're spittin' like two
cats Mary raised her paddle, and for thirty
dollars She got Jacks.

Now that party gal, Babs Johnson
Got obscenely fat Ralph Hansen
And delightedly she got him for a fiver.
She told him, "You can drive my caddy."
"Ah," said he. Kinda like your sugar
daddy." "No, you fool! My designated
driver"

Tom Grove was auctioned off for ten
To build some bookshelves in the den For
librarian Miss Betty Lou McKinney
When I asked him later how the den
looks All filled up with all those books
Tom confessed to me, "She hasn't any."

So, one by one, us boys got auctioned
Except for me and my cousin John
Beatrice Shriver finally took him to tend
her garden
That left three old women gathered
round Like they's buyin' somethin' by the

pound   I smiled at them and held my
ground
One old gal said, "Turn around." "I
beg your pardon!"

"Let's see, I got's two dollar-seventy five."
"I'll take that Billy Small, -- he look alive."
(that was Minny Dee-ancient, aged 85)
Midst all the guffaws, laughin', carrying on
Here I am the very last one
Now I gotta say, I ain't no quitter,
I even tried to outbidder
But, the auctioneer yelled, "Sold!" and looking
down,
Said, "Wha'chu gonna do wi' him Miss Minny?"
"Cain't even pick up yo pot he's so skinny!"
"Oh, I thinks a'lotsa stuff needs gettin' done.
Man aroun 'de house jus' might be fun.
Been a long, long time since I had me one.
Though, I'ze had many."

§ § § §

Oh, by the way, I won ...hands down
I was the talk of all the town
Work? I pulled two rocking chairs around,
and
We spent the week on her front porch talking
All the townfolk drove by, gawking
But I never heard one fella squawking --
Only ladies

Aug. 2015

Little boy, Ben

Then there was that little boy, Ben
He went to school down the block.
He was great in English.....
But then,
But he couldn't count
worth a crock!
Ben was only ten.

oooops, sorry....
Nine.
Let's see,
1,2,3,...
...yup, nine!...

Mar 2014

Mind Over Matter

Aaah, supreme Invention!
Yes! I feel inspired!
It does everything I've desired
And it's genius, I should mention...
I stand to make millions
Maybe even billions!

I do my best thinking verbally!
Confuse them with absurdity!
Oh!... I must submit a prototype!
A Prototype?
Scientific hype!
Gobbledy goop!
Just technical Poop!
After all,
I have a Masters and Doctorate degrees
I can't be bothered with technicalities,
Formalities,
Actualities
while I'm in the midst of ....
...Oh!.... Do you mean I should
actually make a working model of one?
Not really sure it can be done.
But, I'm sure to get the money even if it can't!
I have a government grant!

July 2014

Sunnyside Sam

Let me tell you about Sunnyside Sam
Local hero round Pahrump and
hereabouts–

And yes, he did die,
But while still alive -
You'd best keep some breath fresh'ners out

Now Sunnyside Sam,
Kinda 'Loner' of a man
He lived up out of Pahrump
Bald-headed, be-whiskered, bad- breath and all
Had one good leg, but t'other, just a stump.

His most precious possession,
Most people reckoned
Was his proboscis, his nostrils, his snout --
Whatever it was that old Sunnyside sought
His nose would soon figure it out.

He'd be given a task -
And just sit on his... uh, chair
With his eyes closed and take a deep breath;
We'd all gather round him,
(Provided we're upwind)
Cause his exhale could mean certain death.

Now Sunnyside Sam had a job in the mines...
Worked way down in the hole,
The best in his trade,
Some wagers were made
Cuz he could smell out silver and gold.

Sometime he would crawl,
Bad breath and all
Til you'd think he was leading to hell;
Then he'd stop with a sigh,
Three-four round him would die,
But the rest would enjoy wondrous wealth.

His leg's a sad story -
And just a wee gory
But I'll tell it, if you want to linger,
He was counting past 10,
Trying to impress all the men
An hell, he only had 8-10 fingers.

Well, Sam took to chopping,
Came in the house hopping
Sat down with hammer and nails
His dad shaped a peg;
They created a leg
Been on 'im since – oh,! I'd say he was 12

His name Sunnyside,
Given him by his bride
Stuck through the years since 17,
Seems she glimpsed his whatsit,
Peeping out through the closet--

Oh, we all know she lied,
Says his Sunnyside
Was all that she seen.

His story goes
That she gathered her clothes
And ran naked as bird from the room,
When he turned to peek,
All he saw was her cheek
And Pahrump had a rumor in bloom.

But it's his nose gives him glory,
And I'll tell you that story
How from shysters, he saved the whole state;
Sam smelt'em coming
So he decided on running,
Stood on platform to have a debate.

Some called it justice, some called it fate,
Some called it murder - cold blood;
Sunnyside Sam, why he won the debate
We called it just - Act of God

Died right there on the platform, by gum!
They's all buried up just out of Pahrump.

After retiring, Sam went about hiring
Someone to teach him to yodel and sing
You could hear him from Reno
In the 2 Jack Casino,
All the way up to Warm Springs

That's all he did,
Like some nine year old kid
Tryin' to yodel with all of them warbles
Then one real windy morning
We could hear Sam performing;
When Fred, he started to chortle.

"Listen!" said Fred.
"You hear that?" he said.
"I hear Nothing!" I hollered. "That's right!"
"I don't hear nothin' neither.
Maybe he's taking a breather."
"He's been screeching most all the night."

Well, that morning we found him,
Eight dead coyotes around him,
Fred said "He musta put up one hell of a fight."
But from the look on their faces....
An' hell, they was out 30 paces
Twas his breath, I think, killed em outright.

How the man hisself died,
No one can rightly decide,
But me? Well, I got my ideas.

We all know he was a yodelin',
And a strong wind was a blowin',
And the old boy still had manly vigor;
So how'd he get rigor? -----

He died of an echo, I figure!

It's logical...

**Bald headed,
Bewhiskered,
Bad breath--
And all.**

Mar 2014

<u>*How We Got That Song...*</u>

or Pure Corn......
sorry!

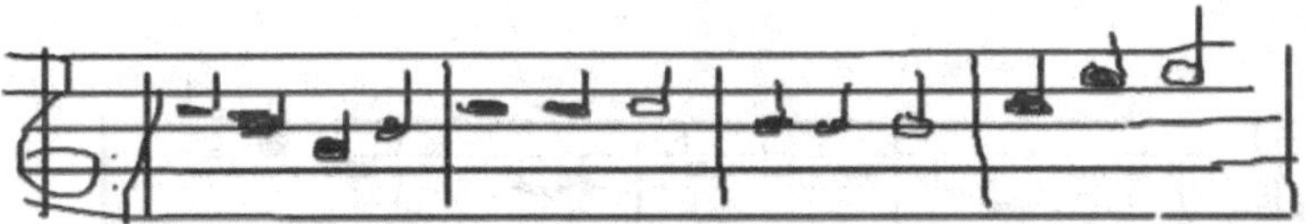

One day we three were going to the
movies
I got permission, Gina got permission,
But Merrilee forgot...
(well, that's what she said).
We were almost at the theatre when
Merrilee's mom came round the bend
in her big Cadillac!
"Quick"! Gina said
"Jump into this rain barrel"!

She did, and we all went 'whew'!
Now we had another problem!
Merrilee was stuck in that rain barrel!
After struggling for five minutes –
The movie had already started –

We tried pulling, yanking,
Turning it upside down!
Finally we gave up and went home.

An hour later, two policemen
Were singing as they brought Merilee home....

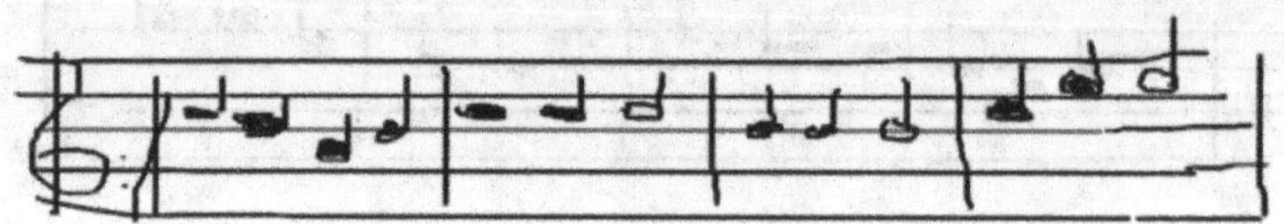

The End

April 2014

A Line in The Dirt

We drew a line in the dirt
then we all took turns
There was Fred, Mickey, Norm,
Tom and me
Didn't matter who went first
everybody knew anyway....
Tom always won.

Then we drew a second line in the dirt
About ten feet away from the first
Like we always did --
same group.
Again, it didn't matter who went first
But this time was different
Any of us could have won
We even made wagers
I won quite a few times

I was a pretty good spitter ....
But nobody could pee like Tom

Mar 2014

<u>The Perfect Blend!</u>

I fill my cup with the second cup
from my morning brew,
leaving a bit still in the carafe--
not enough for even 1/3 cup more,
should I so wish to indulge.

Decision made,
I push the carafe
under the kitchen sink tap and fill the 10 cup jug
almost to the brim;
thus satisfied, I swirl the carafe
around a few times to give it a good rinse
and begin to pour the
rinse water into the sink...

then it strikes me :

this is the perfect blend
for restaurant coffee!

May 2014

Clink.... Clink.....Clink

Clink.....   Clink.....   Clink.....
There! There it is again!
Loud as diesel!
Hammer and cold chisel!
The third time, I think -   maybe four!

Followed by ten minutes of silence!
No one came running!
I thought I'd hear
Footsteps drumming down the floor
As guards raced down the corridor!

Does no one hear?
Does no one come near?

Clink..... Clink..... Clink.....
Now but five minute interval
And again!
Clink..... Clink..... Clink.....
Tension visceral!

Surely, someone must hear!
Someone will come!
Someone *must* come!
Clink.....   Clink.....   Clink.....

Now much shorter!

Clink.....   Clink.....   Clink.....
Clink.....   Clink.....   Clink.....
Flies the mortar!

Now it's continuous!
Clink.....   Clink.....   Clink.....
Clink.....   Clink.....   Clink.....
Clink.....   Clink.....   Clink.....
So conspicuous!
Yet, still the same!
No One Came!
Amost ridiculous!

Ahhhh, At Last!
With that last blast
I see light!
Free by tonight!
Clink.....   Clink.....   Clink.....

Mar 2015

Book Three

Ooops! Wrong Turn!

俳句
SO, WHAT IS HAIKU?
A GROUPING OF
WORDS LIKE THIS
五
七
五
MAKES NO SENSE
TO ME.
言

Haiku

Haiku is a form of poetry developed in Japan. With but three lines, it has a certain syllabolic pattern: 5-7-5. Its structure and essence is to bring oblique thoughts into harmony, but is for me, difficult to wrap my head around. The following are a few attempts --whether correct or not, I leave to experts.

Thoughts spill from my brain
Confidently I plod on --
Tripping over words

Wind in the willows
Toad in his convertible --
Unopened, Unread

Lambing time in spring
Alfalfa and red clover --
Kids are gaining weight

Soaring gracefully
Small gopher looking skyward --
Ah, breakfast at last

Our Father Who Art
We who are about to die
Ask for Your mercy

Clouds float through the skies
Skies stretch to eternity --
Eternity is

~~~~~

Psalm thirty-three, ten
Hopeless are we without God
All the king's horses....

.....And all the king's men
By the size of his army
No warrior escapes

~~~~

Manicured garden
The Dandelion seeds blow --
In hiding 'til spring

Aphids on roses
Invasion of ladybugs --
Aphid mothers weep

Teenage emotions
Age-old -- we can all relate --
Like Lemmings of old

Ah, friend, do not weep
Just tuck a blanket round me --
Fresh and well rested

Do not lean on wood
Fashioned with saw, screws and nails
Lean on wood Maker

Come all! Quench your thirst!
Come to the watering hole --
Beware! Crocodiles!

God watches over
All appears to be at peace --
But tongues kindle flame

Beside me snoring
Windows shaking, dog barking
May be deal breaker

Once upon a time Oh,
I remember it well
Shadows - just shadows

Unsuspecting kids
Bleating their way to be shorn
Just a few more steps

hat lost to the wind
must scurry before the storm
Ah! comes a Pork Pie

Rain, such blessed rain
Rain destroying homes, hillsides -
Rain, such cursed rain!

Bramble and Olive
Watered by the same God --
In Jerusalem

Aug 2014

Book Four

Been Here...
Bunches of Times

Mike ---- The Formative Days -

Hi-- I'm Gonna Be Mike---

Right now I'm havin fun...I think....
Yup! .... Can't talk now......Here I
gooooooooo!
Hey! I can swim! ......Frank! Charles! Mary!
GET OUT of the waaaaaaayyyyyyy!, cuz
HERE I cooooooooooooooome!
Man!...Talk about a headache!.... But I made it.
Shoulda seen all those other tadpoles..
I swam over to them and laughed! Good thing I'm
protected by this bubble......WHEEEEEE..this is
fun!-
HaHa! I won!

Bouncing around in a bubble.... that's all I can
think of for now.... goodbye

It's January..In fact January 17, 1955.....at
exactly 1400 hours.
I know, cuz I heard something with a deep
voice tell something with a soft voice (and it

vibrates)... "Columbia U scientists developed an atomic clock accurate to within one second in 300 years."

..And it just said, "Oh, how nice.".........that's all I can think of for now. Good bye.

<u>Jan 25</u> They're my parents!
I live with mom (that's the one that vibrates), and Dad just visits. He calls me Squirt. Mom doesn't think that's funny. but HE laughs. He tells her stuff and sleeps with her, and then he goes away. stuff like "They just invented scrabble".... and, "There's a new thing called the Nautilus, a atomic submarine..goes underwater." (like me!)
...Yesterday (I think) he bought a telebision.. They watched a new show "Millionnaire" and the American president Ezenhower give the first telebized news conference. Dad says the world will never be the same... he's smart. That's all I can think of for now...

It's February! Dad said that on February 1st, the Bank of Toronto and The Dominion Bank became The Toronto-Dominion Bank. He said he was going to invest in it.
Mom said, that's nice. She was listening to the song <u>_"Sincerely"_</u> on the radio ..says it's the Macguire Sisters.. Dad said, who are they?
I knew that one: Come on DAD..... They're sisters!   ... But, he does know lots of stuff ...
...like, on:
Feb 13, Israel just got 4 of 7 Dead Sea scrolls (somebody must have already ate the other three) ...and on

Feb. 15th, 1st pilot plant to produce man-made diamonds.
Mom said she was going to invest in that. She's smart, too...(I wonder how many diamonds you can get off each pilot plant??) _Sincerely_ has been playing on the radio for ten weeks...... that's all I can think of.

NOW we're into March! _"Sincerely"_ has been replaced by _"Love me Tender"_ ..Some guy on the radio all the time..and then even on tv tonight for the first time. Mom wants to see what he looks like. Dad likes the news. Mom gets sick a lot. Dad says she'll be even sicker after tonight..... I'm left in the dark... that's all I can think of.....

March 4   News out of Israel about problems in
Gaza.... wherever that is... almost 50 people killed.. Dad says this has been going on for generations... other news they sent a facsimile all the way across the continent on the radio! I don't know what that means but dad says it's important. But he says they sent pictures on a telephone line, in Washington, D.C.—way back on Oct 3, 1922....Dad is smart. Mom said she liked Elvis..... then we went to the bathroom and she vomited. ... I thought I was done for.... that's all I can think of for now.

It's April..Nothing happened in March except a new tv program called Davy Crockett.
Dad says can you imagine watching a show where a guy has a animal tail hanging over his eyes

oh, yeah, there was a riot in the
streets of Montreal.

I guess some hockey player named "Rocket" hit
somebody and got suspended for the whole
year.

Dad said the guy deserved getting hit and Mom
said can you imagine grown men wearing skates
carrying clubs and beating a little piece of rubber
all over the ice.

...Dad didn't think it was funny,.... but mom and
I laughed.... Dad said the big news of March was
the formation of Chase Manhattan bank merging
from 3 really big banks.. I don't know how big it
is .... but then... I don't know how big anything
is.... ..

And now it's April _"Cherry Pink and Apple
Blossom White"_ by Prez Prado is on the radio.... I
was listening to Duffy's Tavern when she turned
the dial..."Hello this is Duffy's Tavern..Archie
doin' the talkin" ...he's crude.. I know, cause mom
says......
and lots has happened this month................like,
Ray Crock started a little restaurant in
California in the states called MacDonalds . He
says he's gonna sell 100 hamburgers a day. Mom
says she might invest in his fast food experiment.
Dad just laughed and said it should be called
"Eat our food or fast: a healthy choice "
Winston Churchill got real old and resigned
this month, and a doctor Salk invented a polio
vaccine ... boy!.. mom and dad are happy !.......
but
Dad got really mad at the tv when
the Detroit red wings beat the

Montreal Canadiens for the
stanley cup.
Dad said they stole it.
Mom said she had one in the cupboard if they
needed it that bad, and well,
...I'm with mom...and that's all I know .....
Oh yeah, I almost forgot.. Einstein died on the
18th.
Mom said he was brilliant.
One of her favorite things that he said *was "I
have no special talent. I am only passionately
curious."*
I think when I grow up, I'm gonna be a Einstein.
Dad was reading the newspaper, and he read
that the first "Walk"- "Don't Walk" lighted street
signals were just installed in some city
somewhere. I was just thinking that Einstein
must have invented them when mom said
whoever came up with that idea never lived in
Montreal. Now I'm not sure...
Hi...It's May and I'm getting bigger!
And Mom isn't puking all the time!
Talk about a confined space when she was doing
that!
Dad says all of Europe is abuzz with treaties
and signing of peace pacts.
The Warsaw pact, Nato, West Europe Union
established...
and all
the while the US is testing nuclear bombs in
Nevada and in the Pacific Ocean.
I heard Dad tell mom that Mickey Mantle just hit
a whole buncha homeruns of over 500 feet,
and Willy Shoemaker won the Kentucky Derby
on a horse named Swaps,

and Rocky Marciano beat Don Cocknell in 9 for
heavyweight boxing title.
Mom said that's nice, and did he know that
the Presbyterian Church decided to let women be
ministers. I didn't hear his answer, cuz Amos'n'
Andy just came on the radio,
and I started getting the hiccups,
and discovered I can blow bubbles!

But I stopped ...
just in time to hear her say that in the
states, Eisenhower and the Supreme Court
have decided that the schools be racially
integrated immediately.
And Now Britain is in Crisis .....
a Rail strike has shut down everything..
I heard Sapphire say "GEORGE KINGFISH
STEVENS!" and him say, "Awwwwwwww,
Sapphire, Honey....."
That's all I can think of...._It's cherry pink and
Apple blo.....zzzzzzzzzz"_

June 7 ... Mom and Dad are watching a new tv
show ....$64,000.00 question...I don't think Dad is a
Einstein.....that's all I can think of,.........oh, except
there's another new song out... really, really
fast... It's called
'Rock around the Clock"...
Dad doesn't like it, but
mom and I dance sometimes when he's gone and
she turns the radio up really, really, really loud
when that song comes on .

It's almost July. WE got _Color TV!_ (I think
that means integrated--probably another
Supreme Court decision) We.... well,

dad and mom
watched the president of the US give a speech
in color!
We also went to see a new movie: _The Lady and
The Tramp_ by Walt Disney.
Mom and dad both liked it...I just went along for
the ride.
In the news this month (I'm getting more
passionately curious all the time...like Einstein)
Pope Pius XII ex-communicated Juan Peron in
Argentina...I don't know what that means, but I'm
curious ... and in Illinois, people gotta put on seat
belts when they drive a car.. mom says no
pregnant woman could ever do that! ... I agree..
we got that news on our color tv set!

It's July..we're watching a lot of TV. Mom says
we'll go blind. HUH! I'm already blind! I can't see
a thing! But there's the Johnny Carson Show,
and a music show called Lawrence Welk.
Mom says it comes with bubbles, so maybe he
hiccups. The music is ok, but I still like _Rock
around the clock_ best It's been #1 for 7 weeks
and still great!
About the only two items of news are: that the
guy who made the movie _Lady and The Tramp_
has just opened up a kids' park out in the country
in Orange County, California. hoping to make
big money. He calls it Disneyland. And now, by
law, every coin in the United states must say " In
God we trust".

That's important to somebody, I guess... that's all
I can think of. Wait wait!   ....
I can wiggle my toes! And my elbows!

In fact, Dad told a joke the other day.
I'll tell it to you.
Mom was saying that she enjoys
flower arranging.... and dad said, you can lead a
horticulture but you can't force her to get an
education. Mom didn't think that was funny, but
dad laughed, ..so I laughed too, and I accidently
elbowed mom..and well, THAT'S how I found
out..... about moving my elbows I mean..........

The minimum wage in the states has been raised.
It happened yesterday, August 12. goes from $0.75
to $1.00 for a hour. I'm ready to go to work, Boy!

When dad comes home from work now we
already know the news. It's on our new color tv.
Hurricane Diane struck August 19 and killed over
200 in NE US and became the most costly storm
ever with over a billion dollars in damage...
    "<u>AINT THAT A SHAME</u>" is on the radio.... I like
FATS Domino, better than Pat Boone.....,....... and
there's a new book out that mom says I'm gonna
be in someday...It's called the Guinness Book of
World Records.

Boy is it getting _cramped_ in here.. Mom! have you
not heard of stretching exercises? I can just hear
Walter Winchell:••• *"Good morning*
America and all the ships at sea:••• boy crammed
into world's smallest room." ••

SEPTEMBER.... things are so confusing...It's
gotta be TV.... I'm trying to take it all in with my
passionate curiosity, but there's just too much
stuff...
I'll just capsulate it for you: GET IT? Capsulate?

ooops, sorry mom...
Anyway.......t's September 10
"Gunsmoke" premieres on TV....great reviews!
(Mom likes Chester......Dad just stares at Miss
Kitty.. at least that what mom says)

Then on Sept. 19, Hurricane Hilda, killed 200 in
Mexico ...   also, on Sept. 19
After heavy shelling of docks and Oil Refinerys
at Buenes Aires - led by combined army and
navy revolt, Argentine president
Juan Peron, resigns, flees to Paraguay.
Then, on the 21st, Rocky Marciano KOs Archie
Moore in 9 to retain heavyweight crown.
Then the next day, Hurricane Janet kills 500 in
Caribbean ..and on the 28th of September
1st World Series color TV broadcast on NBC-TV !
Dad says he can't imagine TV in black and
white anymore.. HA! ASK ME!
I can't even imagine TV!
Oh, then on the 29th of September "Sergeant
Preston," debuts on CBS ..

"ON KING! On you Huskies!" When I grow up
I'm gonna be a mountie... Then a newscaster like
John Cameron Swayze, and then a ... and THEN
a Einstein.......... or
....a fireman!
Whew!
This month is finally over ....I'm pooped!.... get
it, mom? Ooops! sorry mom. (Damn elbow!)
Ooops! Again! ..... (One of dad's words....wonder
if they heard me say that?)

Hey, now it's October!
Today is Oct. 1   Dale Carnegie died today. Dad

**told mom, He's the guy that said, When life deals
you a lemon, make lemonade......
(I wonder if he was talking about me????)**

"Honeymooners" premiered tonight......dad really
likes this one... mom thinks it's crude... "to the
Moon, Alice!" (....Dad wants a 2nd tv.......)
And TWO really good shows premiered on the
same day - Oct.3:
"Captain Kangaroo" premiered on CBS-TV, 'Good
Morning, Captain!"
Also, the "Mickey Mouse Club" went on the air!
Whoo Hooo!

It's Oct 4!
Bronx Bombers win Series - beat Yanks in 7
and again the same day, Rev Sun Young Moon
leaves prison in Seoul....... Dad says he's
a loonie. He met him in an airport on a business
trip.
It's October 6.   LSD is made illegal in US.   Is
nothing sacred ?
Next, giving birth will be made obsolete!

Hey! Enough!
Stop with the squeezing! What the ....?   Hey,
where'd my swimming pool go? Hey mom! Stop it
I tell you.... Hey! What's the rush?
No! NO I tell you no! I'm not budging! I've still
got a few good months........
HEY! HEY,.........................

HEY! ....I CAN SEE!
I SEE A LIGHT!... No, a TUNNEL! NO!... A
TUNNEL , <u>AND</u> A LIGHT!
THIS IS COOL. HEY! This is freaky! ALRIGHT!
I'm INTO THIS! COME ON, MOM! PUSH! You
heard the doc!............ PUSH!
HERE I COOOOOOOOOME! ....
M - I - C - K - E - Y !
SO, MOM, What's for dinner?

for
Mike
Oct 2005 on his 50th Birthday

These next three little reminisces are addressed to my brother--we were always quite close--so I tried to send him a rhyme as his birthday approached...to make sure he knew that I reached out to him, even when our philosophies clashed at times---blood, as they say.....

<u>Bro - at Fifty-Nine</u>

Well, young feller ...
         ...So you're one short o sixty,
          An' still feelin' frisky,
While roamin' the Carribee-ann...
          Just one shy o sixty
          An' one shot o whisky
To make you feel 30 again...

Take stock o surroundin's
An' don't let the houndin's
Of Gov'nmint officers rile
Or cause you to worry....
Or be in a hurry
While seekin' your gold in the Isle

Now you ain't no miner
'Cause no '59r
Made history strugglin' for dust
But sure is for certain
That my body's hurtin'
At our age... huh!
Thank God we don't rust.

One more til you're 60
An' not quite so frisky
But, don't think for a moment
You're through;

Don't squander the gold
That's there in the hold...
The "Refiner" is countin' on you;
He'll sip from your cup
An' weigh it all up,
An' hopefully relish the brew.

just a mere child -
Feb 1999

Sesenta Nueve!

Well, well now, Ol' Timer, you've made it this far.
Without bein' funny..... twas it birdie or par?
Ya still a Spring Chicken, or been through th' war?
Ya runnin? Or limpin? Yore teeth in a jar?
Are ye smellin' the roses - or be they too bloody far?
Ah............... Sesenta Nueve!

Ain't seen ya fur ages, but spect we're still kin -
Still think about ya --whar ye be, whar ye bin,
And sometimes I worry, cuz ye know what they say
Just so many minutes - then it's back to the clay -
Shore like to think I'll still see you one day,
Ah.............. Sesenta Nueve!

Oh, I know what yur thinkin' - thet time is a'wastin'
That mind's all wound up with it's hastin' an' hastin'
Searchin' for gold an' cummin' up tin
The Spirit be willin' - the flesh a mite thin

An' maybe those treasures ain't fittin' to win
Ah............... Sesenta Nueve!

Me? I'm pokin' retirement with a shortenin' stick
Gonna stretch out in Hemet - no, not much of a
pick,
But the livin' is cheap - an' the needs are but few
Might even be a place there for you
We could wax eloquent or just "pick out a few"
Ah............... Sesenta Nueve!

Feb 1, 2009

*[...Written to my brother as he turned 69, and was
just flapping about -- I invited him to join me in my
winter digs in Hemet, California-- he declined. I
suppose each of us reaches for a particular star]*

This last poem to my brother was unfortunately, my last one to him --
I wrote it not as a prophecy, but as a sobering consideration - to all of us who have reached the seventy year threshold -- that "Hoary head" phase in our lives -- By phone we spoke of the ticks -- Of goals, accomplishments, unfinished business... In June we had a good conversation concerning some music he was working on, and two days later, he was gone ... So, indeed, as this poem says, "handle with care."

Chronos Visits at 74

Handle with care:

2,333,664,000
Ticks thus far
You've been given:

Ah!
See!
How the Master
Chronos
Winds
One so driven! ...
So much to do,
So little time!

And yet (You must say....)
"2,333,
664,000
Precious ticks,
And they were mine...."

The Writer, Sage
In an earthy crust ---
Each tick must shine
Free of dust!

May the Master Chronos
Wind just right
Not too slack,
Not too tight

Perhaps,
Because we're only clay
Perhaps,
We have just ticks away,
then gone ---
Or,

Perhaps

3-500 million Added ticks
You'll been given;
Ticks, ticks, ticks Anon ...

Bundled
2,333,
664,000
Documented...
Filed away.

**May Chronos teach
Each tick a
precious
moment in time -----**

Handle with care!

February 2014

Elliott at 39

It was '73,
18 September
A date I surely will remember
I think twas 5PM, but maybe 6 or 7
Lights were low, soft music playin' -

Mary K. was called and came
Of course the doctor did the same....
Propped up in bed and sipping wine,
Comfortable, and feeling fine,

Sue with me, the doc and Mary
Not your normal "cash and carry".

Doc said, "A birth like this is never read
In books - no stirrups, hospital bed -
No nurse, forceps, sterile smell;
Just peace and calm and 'all is well"

And so with that, Doc cut the cord
And my son Elliott, you were born.
Now here we are, 39 years hence
'Most 4 decades comes, lad, from thence.
Yes, much has happened in those years -
'Tween birth an' Sierra Nevada beers

Some things I'm sure You'd rather not remember
Since you first came forth that mid- September
Once your hair all disappeared
Made a statement – "Yeah, Look at me, I'm
weird!"

AC/DC, Metallica, Music ? NOISE !
But Typical of lots of boys

Moved a bit with Mom,--- then Dad -
Swung on ropes with Lee McNabb
Old women threatened to call the police,
As you dragged poor Ralph across the street.

Oh, and then (almost forgot)
Then you worked the old Man's shop
" Go do this hack out, Sweep the floors, clean the
latrine
Stop Belly-aching ! Pay's the same ---
Buck an hour—now ain't that sweet ?
And of course, "All the glass that you can eat...."

Sat on Abe Lincoln for Uncle Sam -
Off Somalia, China, Vietnam.
"All Hands on deck!"?? Not this young Buck
Mountains might bring better luck...

Ah, Yosemite !-- Tranquil!   Water! Peace!
Like the song says, "I have been Released!"

Back to hard work, vacation over
Worked a while for some Aptos drover
All the while learning, learning
But to again be free you were ever-yearning

You and Beth, with her dad's debenture
Sallied forth with your own venture Ah,
the Entrepreneurial Spirit beckons
And born was your "Artistic Reflections"

Not yet quit from signed entangles
But "Bond to Free"--- The carrot dangles

Your Apprenticeship card will soon be met
Your Journeyman ticket paid with sweat
And just as sure as Yosemite
Beckoned you : tranquility

Your "stickability" makes me proud
Using tools that God endowed
Ever onward, Elliott my son
Life's Journey has only just begun

And so, to You, as you near 2 score
I raise my glass : "To three score more !"

Pop, 2012

JUST ANOTHER DAY

B ut wait... Didn't seem that way-
No, not at the time --
Not with Dr. Langenheim...

"Sure, I will house call—and deliver --"
(Just looking at her made one quiver ----
German - Tall as Amazon she was),
"But, Only If you take Lamaze!"
In broken English she went on---
"Baby does not turn, you come downtown!
Baby turn - other way around."

L : "Do you know what can happen if a
complicated birth?"
S : "My Naturals are the easiest ones on earth --
No Drugs, or needles, episiotomies."
L. : "And Just How Many have you Seen?"
S : "Uh.................I've seen one," said Mother Queen

Now the babe was upside down and breech,
Her butt could split S like a peach!
But S felt bubbles in her tummy
Babe was turning just for mummy!

So this Amazon, one Langenheim
Came to our house—and just in time.
Black satchel full of tools: knife and such
Dropped to the floor in front of us...

"Don't push! Stay cool and breathe Lamaze!"
Oh sure--ha-uh-ha-uh-ha-uh ha uh-ha-uh ha-uh-
ha
(who's kidding whom? Gotta push! ha-uh-ha-uh)
I whispered, "PUSH!" as I held my wife --
Langenheim whirled then, with her knife --
L: "I ordered - not to push!" as infant cried;
S: "Oh I tried, I really tried!"

L: "Oh, I suppose it's not so bad;
You only split up just a tad --
Won't need to stitch you up with thread --
Just stick a diaper on the bed --
God will heal the tear," she said.

Babe, by this time, almost out;
We knew now who we fussed about.
Screaming, crying, a wee young sprite
Recognizable on sight!
I glanced down at this little ball of noise
Sighed, "Life's much easier with boys."
" $200," said Langenheim.

Oh, I haggled a bit, then muttered, "fine!"
Worth it? Hell, yes! A Thousand times!
"L" grabbed her bag and counted twice,
An' disappeared into the night.

**JUST ANOTHER DAY ? Don't think so, Mack.
A special day, say I, in fact.**

**Since Lorinda came –and I add no frills -
forty-some years ago in Tara Hills
She's been a joy, unique!
Special!   Ok,...... weird!
(uh, well, Just a tad),
Makes me proud to be her dad.**

Pop - 2012

<u>*We see Alyssa At Seventeen*</u>

Oh, it was bound to happen See,
it happens to us all....
Could be any time of year
Winter, summer, fall
Could even be on the date itself
Although with most, unlikely
So we store our thoughts upon a shelf
And wait for it, politely.

The thing that makes her so unique
Is what's been put inside her
For what's in - comes out - so to speak
So, how well did we guide her ?

Took several years-all in the past,
Spent all of her life much younger
But Alyssa's SEVENTEEN at last!
And has this grownup hunger!

As parents, grandparents, uncles, aunts
We join in celebration
And through this year and its events
Let's beam with satisfaction!

Maturity is *mind* and *heart!*
That's what scriptures say,
Make today the determined start -
With change from youth to Lady

See, your age is not a circled date
On a calendar somewhere
But the sum of every thought and trait -
That brings you to <u>where YOU are</u>!

Congratulations, Young Lady!

Summer 2015

Book Five

Sounds of

Young'uns

AHEAd!

(Big'uns An' little'uns

Harry And the Lightning Bugs

arry saw some little lights a'flying in the
park
     And wondered how they flew;
He held Dad's hand (cuz it was dark)
     So he asked Dad if he knew.

"No, I'm not sure, son," Dad replied...
     "They're bugs, is all I know,
And sometimes in the summer nights
     Their butts begin to glow."

"Their butts?" said Harry, with a laugh,
     "Dad, do their butts get hot?"
"Well, let's catch a few, examine them
     Then we'll know If they do or not."

"What do people call these bugs, Dad?
     I'm sure they have a name."
"Yes, they call them fireflies or lightning bugs;
     They're all one and the same."

"Dad, why did God put their light
On their butt and not their head?
They can't see where they're going
Only where they've been, instead."

"Oh, Harry, I think it's just to let their friends
Know it's safe to fly tonight
And maybe too, it might be when they're happy
They become more bright."

"Then I'm not going to catch them, Dad
I'll just watch the flying light.
'You fireflies, Glow! Be happy!
It's safe to fly tonight!'"

So, watching done, this man and son
Walked homeward in the dark;
They went upstairs and said their prayers --
Harry prayed of nothing save his new friends in
the park.

He prayed, "God you do some funny things,
Some folks would think You're nuts
To build some bugs – 'mosquito size'
With flashlights on their butts.
Amen."

April 2012

Harry Builds a Birdhouse

In Dad's workshop Harry stared up at all the
tools hanging in neat rows.
"Dad, do all these tools have special jobs? --
like these and these and those?"

As Harry pointed at each tool, Dad named them
one by one -
A hammer, drill, chisel, wrench, screwdriver,
staple gun.

"Yes, Harry, special tools for special jobs – there
are many more than these...
If you have proper tools to do a job,
It goes quick as a breeze."

"Do we have proper tools to build a birdhouse
Dad? I sure hope we do"
Harry got excited then, and Dad was smiling, too.

"Why, sure, of course---.
But let's not get the cart before the horse!"

"Before you start on any job, Son, you must first
have a plan –
Here ! Take this piece of paper, I'll help you with
ideas
We'll draw the house the way you want, and
figure how big it is.

Will this be a single family home, with just one
dad and mother?
Or do you want a multiplex, to share it with some
others?"

"Dad, you're funny!" Harry laughed, and thought
about bird neighbors..
Like : "Hi, we're having worms for lunch..
Would you care to join us later?"
No thank you Mrs Robin, we already ate."

He was still daydreaming away when he heard
his father say:
"Be creative Harry, And it's ok to make mistakes.
That's why we have erasers, and sometimes a
pencil breaks."

So Harry drew, then erased, and then again he
drew ----
With a pencil - a Dixon Ticonderoga #2

"Just how tall will be its walls?   Now think
about the floor....
"That's great, Harry! Ummm, maybe just a tad bit
more!"

"Oh,oh--- what about a door?"
"A door?" asked Harry in disbelief. "I'll just make
a hole."
"Birds don't need a door do they? Do you think
they get cold?"

"You're right, you're right, Harry, my mistake. A
little wee hole is good.
Now let's just check out everything and then go
get the wood.

We'll add some measurements to your plans –
they're what's called dimensions;
That way we'll make it real exact, and build to
your intentions."

And although Dad did the sawing up,
Harry did the 'portant stuff.
Dad showed him how to use the vise
To make the corners come out nice;

And overhang the roof a ways
To keep birds dry on rainy days.
With a gap in the boards on one of the sides
In case it got too hot inside.

Oh! the workshop "buzzed" and "thunked" and
"hummed"....
(Yes! Harry had safety goggles on!)
And a half hour later they were done....

Dad nailed it to the barn door frame
... And in less than a week some finches came

And Harry? He had loads of fun!
In fact, He's thinking of building another one.

Sept 2014

Harry Struggles With Yesterday

On a bar stool Harry sat, while his Dad
was fixing lunch.
"Is it Peanut Butter and Jam again?-
Yup! I had a hunch."
Well, Harry wasn't really sitting -- twirling says it
better --
Dad said, "Harry, get a napkin. Don't want jam on
your new sweater."

So Harry took one final spin, and slid down to the
floor.
"Sure thing, Dad," and grabbed a few and
brought his dad one more.
"Dad, I was just thinking: what happened to
yesterday?
I mean, we ate the same old sandwich that we're
eating here today..."

His dad gave Harry a funny look as he climbed
back on the stool,
And watched him munch all round the crust, as if
that were a rule.
"Well, son, that's a good question." And Harry's
father rubbed his chin...
"It's much more simple than it seems, I mean, if
you can take it in."

(Munch, Munch)   "Oh, I can take it in, Dad," said
Harry with a grin.
(Crunch, Crunch) "Dad, I'm almost 5 you know; I
can take it in."
(And the stool began to spin.)

"We---ll," said Dad, "do you remem........."
"Wait Dad! I know what you're going to say.
I remember the lightning bugs at play!. And I
know that was yesterday!
But Hey! Are they still there? *(Munch, Munch)*
And if not, then where?"
Did yesterday just 'get up and go somewhere'?

"Wow, Harry! That kind of thinking is called
profound!"
And Harry beamed brightly as the stool twirled
around.

"Well, Harry, you ate a Peanut Butter and Jam
sandwich yesterday, agreed?"

**And you are enjoying a different one today, I
see...**

**"Well, Dad, Duh! laughed Harry. You made it!"
So, where did the other sandwich go?"
"Dad, that's silly. You know! I ate it!"**

**"Exactly! Once it's gone it doesn't come again.
Just like yesterday—it was here ---but now, it's
like it's never been."**

**"Except, Dad," Harry said thoughtfully, "Except
for memories."
"PROFOUND!" said Harry's dad, ardently.
"PROFOUND!" said Harry, happily...
Wiped the jam from off his chin,
And gave the stool another spin.**

--- *June 2015*

Miss Butterfly in Thyme

Once upon a thyme
Miss Butterfly sat
Preening herself in the sun;

Coming along, then,
Chattering Mr. and Mrs. Wren
Each one
Chewing on a cinnamon bun

"Why are your wings spread out so?"
They wanted to know
As she sat for a time
On the thyme.

"My wings are still wet
They haven't dried yet
See, I've just crawled out of my hole."

"You've been down in a hole?
Down there with Sir Mole?"
Mr. Wren dropped his bun from his beak.

Mrs. Wren started to chatter
Dropped her bun; but it didn't matter
"Mr. Mole doesn't ever speak."

"No! my hole's a cocoon,
My own special room,
There's no one else in it but me."

"My Goodness! Such chatter!
But really ! No matter,
I once was a worm, you see."

"A worm!" She heard Mr. Wren say,
"We could have had a full meal...
We settled for the cinnamon bun deal!"

Not wishing to hear more
From this chattering bore,
Miss Butterfly sighed, "Please go home;
I need some thyme on my own."

April 2014

Accumulating Frogs

Herbert lay dreaming on his bed
Holding his head --

He frowned.
And though he slept so very sound
He knew what lay in store;
He'd had these headaches oft' before.

It all started very small...
Almost nothing at all,
Like the gentle lap, lap, lapping
Of some tree-lined mountain lake;
Each little wave was slap, slap, slapping...
And a whisper sound the trees did make.

Or perhaps it's not a wave at all;
Perhaps a bouncing rubber ball.

Lush meadows full of frogs and flowers...
But the flowers started clap, clap, clapping!
He covered up his ears and whined.

Green and Yellow Frogs were Hopping
Everywhere on Herbert's Bed

Now green and yellow frogs were yapping,
The whispering trees all started laughing,
And worst of all came ice cold showers ...
All this he pictured in his mind.

Now 200 dancing Fairies came --
Prancing up and down his brain;
But they didn't use their feet at all
They bounced in on those rubber balls!
"Oh, Sure!", he thought, "You're having fun ...
But please bounce off those Kettle Drums!"

Boom! Boom! Boom!
(These Fairies weren't too kind....
The noises filled poor Herbert's mind) --
Showers turned to icy rain
And flooded Herbert's weary brain,
His headache pained, his patience drained --
He bolted upright and exclaimed:

"See Here! Scram! Get out! Leave me be!
Your meadow lakes, your clapping flowers,
Your noisy drums and trees and showers
Yes, your bouncing rubber balls,
Leave me be, and take them all!

I HAVE A HEADACHE! Can't you see?"
And with that, he grabbed a Fairie --
-- looked her in the eye,

"Why can I not simply dream without a
headache?"
"Why? -- At least go away and let me try!"

And as she passed by she kicked his bed --
"Humph to you!" is all she said;

But she sprinkled him with Fairie dust
(A thing that every Fairie must) --

Now with Fairie dust you sleep like a log
And Herbert mumbled through his groggy fog:
"Oh ...you can leave the frogs."

Jan 2015

The Farmer and the Ax

HELP, HELP!
Somebody Help!
Cried the rooster,
As the farmer came,
Wielding an ax

"Oh, Moo! Boo Hoo!" cried the Cow
"Oh, Cluck! Such luck!" cried the hen
"Oh, Bow Wow! Yooowwl!" cried the hound
"Oh, OOOOINKKKKK!" Cried the sow
"Oh, Neigh! NeigHHHH!" cried the horse
"Oh, I, I, I, I, I, I, I'll take a drumstick...."
stuttered the cat.

April 2014

The Night Thunder and Lightning Double-Dared

Young Frank was sitting on a stool
In the parlor (or the den),
And Cat came o'er to join him –
Young Frank was only ten.
Cat whisked his tail and rubbed Frank's leg,
"Cat, you came over just to beg?"
Frank reached out and scratched Cat's chin.

Thunder snapped across the sky,
The door swung wide, and with a cry
Frank's sister Jen, just six this week,
Raced in the room, and with a shriek
Said, "Frank, Frank ! Where can I hide?"
Something terrible is happening outside!
Oh, please don't let it in!"

The Lightning flashed, and Thunder roared
And Jen cried out in fear;
Frank laughed, "You should see yourself --
Go look in that big mirror."

And so she did, and made a face --
"It's not so bad," she said-
"Now I will not be afraid."

Frank stopped scratching Cat's stuck-out chin,
And with approval, the young lad grinned.
Jen looked again, and again she made a face;
"Every time we have a storm I'll try to be real
brave;
See ? I'll look in the mirror, I'll be a clown!
Make a funny face, jump up and down,
And wave."

Jen stepped away from the great mirror
That leaned against the wall;
But terror tried to come again
As Lightning bolt lit up the hall.
Frank, of course, showed little fright;
Cat perhaps: just a wee mite,
But Jen – why, not at all!

And true to word, Jen's tongue stuck out
And her finger pushed her nose;
Oh, Thunder clapped, she screamed aloud,
But tongue and nose stayed froze...
And then she laughed, a great big laugh,
"See Frank, I'm not scared!"
I beat them, Lightning and Thunder both,
Although they double-dared.

July 2013

The Lonely Troll

A long time ago
  (Just where I don't know)
   There lived a young troll
  Named Billy

Who had nothing to eat,
He had dirty feet,
Of course he lived
Under a bridge,
Silly!
(he's a troll—remember?)

Had only a bunk-bed
Stove and a fridge
Yes! He had running water
He lived under a bridge!... (duh)

He had no one to frighten
Threaten or scare
No one walked over
So he couldn't charge fare

When he went to the store
For rotten potatoes
The storekeeper's daughter
Threw fresh, red tomatoes

He looked in the mirror,
Hmmm, maybe too clean.
He wallowed in slime
And then looked again

That's better, he thought
Now I'm dirty enough
Now townfolks will come
I look like a scruff!

A truck rumbled up
And stopped on the bridge
Two men leaned o'er the rail,
Then threw down an old fridge.

Then came 3 computers,
A broken umbrella,
A dozen cell phones,
Meat with salmonella

A 60" T.V.,
Some Itch powder for feet
He salvaged at least
The umbrella and meat.
He already had an old fridge remember?
(Silly)

Dust and debris covered his face,
His hair and his shoulders
Delirious Billy!
Oh, he was in clover!

Three more trucks rumbled on top
Garbage and refuse: kerplop! Kerplop!
Were tossed off the bridge
Created sort of a ridge
Beneath the bridge.

And then,
One day it was over.....
Well,......sorta over
Kinda, sorta.......
Kinda ....paved over

That ridge
Beneath the bridge
Became I-5!

Is Billy still alive?

WHAT?
That's silly....
He was a troll.....
(*But still, nobody knows!*)

April 2014

Book Six

Musings In A Maze

Maple Leaf in Moonlight

I watch the maple leaf --
black against the shimmering water,
making its way down the brook,
sometimes catching the rays of moonlight --
turning orange, yellow and black again;
swirling in the eddies --
occasionally picking up swifter current...

And, captured
in the reflection of that moment,
I think of you --
your flowing hair, the surprise in your face
at sudden shifts, twists, turns
that life throws at us --
yes, us.
The 'us' who had everything!

Lifeless now, barely moving
yet moving away --
away from the us that was --
the only remaining thing is the memory,

But even that
now circles wearily
as it meanders away from me
to disappear just like the maple leaf
caught in the brackish downward swirl.

Sept 2015

<u>Graphite</u>

In shades of monotones –
Varying nuances of
perceived color...
Yet without hue
Nature unintentioned.

Billowing skyward,
Settling in streaks
Of varying degree --
Filtering, disappearing,
In occasional wisps –
Blacks and greys on o'erhead canvas ...

Graphite!

Why?
Oh, why does the formation not congeal?
Why does it ever dissipate?
Why does the *Artist* not bring forth
Vibrant hue, color,
Brightness?

Why that grey seems my lot ?
Why am I ever living
In this morass of nebula?

Graphite......
Damnable Graphite!

12/12/2013

There Is A River

The Man took me to the Temple door

I started to ask Him, "Whatever for?"
. ... Then I saw water trickling from under...
What is all this I wonder

Just a trickle did I behold...
bubbling up from 'neah threshold.
He said, "Follow me,
And you will see."

Now, the entrance to the temple
Stood perfect toward the east.
And the water, just a dribble
Made damp our sandalled feet

Neath the south side of the temple,
It hardly made a ripple
But it meandered toward the East.

Then he led me through the northern gate
and around to the outer --
And toward the East
Water bubbled forth as well --
This flow was toward the South.
He said, "What are your thoughts, Ezekiel?"
But I opened not my mouth.

Then He said, "Come, friend, let's walk."

And so, we as it trickled followed that slight
flow; Eastward, as we walked and talked,

That trickle began to grow....

Now He held in hand a measuring line,
Where it came from I don't know
But, He measured off a one third mile
Along that shallow, meandering flow

Stretched out in front on either side
Was lifeless along our trail
Barren, dusty, plain and wide
And in some places, shale.

He said, "Step in the water - go across;
Would you say it's flowing?"
"Why, it's ankle deep!" I was at a loss --
"Not only that," I cried, "but growing!"

"Look behind, friend, at the banks
Tell me what you see."
I stared in wonder! "To God be thanks!"
Lush, grasses! Greenery!

"Is this mirage? -- Am I in a dream?"
He simply looked at me and smiled,
We were walking now, along a stream,
For another one third mile;

I looked behind - from whence we'd come
Nothing back there looked the same;
I saw flowers, grasses, even trees!
We crossed once more - Twas to our knees!

We walked further, toward the east
The waters? Yes! They did increase
When we'd reached another one third mile
My Friend and I, we stopped a while...

"This water shall persist to flow;
Through desert places it shall go...
Through the Jordan Valley to the east
All the way to the Dead Sea."

We then, my Friend and I
Crossed...swirling water to my thigh.
Do you think this may be yet a dream?
You see ahead, behind, you've seen,
Everything which once was dead
Now lives!
Oh, man, what are your thoughts on this?

Come! We've yet one more bit to go.
Then it's homeward to the source."
Ah, Yes! The Temple, but of course ...
The Cause and purpose of this flow!
My Friend has taught me! Now I know!

The sting of death has run its course,

Confronted by this great Life-Force
And so, on our journey one more third
I walked, amazed, without a word

The flow, by now, a roaring current
No way to ford this raging torrent.
"Ah, my friend, are you impressed?"
Inside I quaked, and answered, "Yes!"

So we returned along the banks
And as we walked, we offered thanks.
Now trees were standing, yielding fruit
Where just before ne'er trunk nor root
Where not a blade of grass did shoot!
Life Giver ...
this mighty river!

"You saw the flow from whence we came;
Now to the South, it's just the same
This flow will reach the Dead Sea, friend,
Where signs of life have never been;
But, instead of salt and death
This stream will turn the waters fresh.

Ezekiel, can you just envision?
Do you believe that this will happen?
Anything this river touches will be healed?
Completely real!

No fable, friend.
From En Gedi to En Eg-laim
Fishers will stand along the shore,
Nets spread out -- like ne'er before --
Fishing waters, now completely teeming!

Where the river flows,
it brings new life-
Fruit trees grow
On either side
From the Temple, yea,
To far and wide,
And the leaves will be for healing.

Now Ezekiel, My friend
I'll give to you my iron pen
You write it down from start to end
With ardor, zeal, fervent feeling.

Spare no tittle, leave no jot!"
And to my best, I have not!

[Adapted from
Scripture Ezekiel 47]

Oct 2015

Perhaps, Perhaps Not!

Reddish brown - bright, somewhat
smooth
Somewhat round
Half-buried in the sand
Pulled it from the bubbly brook; sat down
On the sandy ground
Studied it in my hand

Where have you been, bright little rock?
A distant star?
Fragment of a meteor -- far from here?
A flash, A flame!
And you appear?
Perhaps.... perhaps not.

Did you crash down from a craggy cliff?
Were you born a boulder ..?
(when you were much, much older.)
Then rain, wind and snow,
And of course, the water's flow
Shed you of the minerals and mass?
Until you wound up in my hand at last?
Perhaps.... perhaps not.

David, as a lad, picked up a stone like you;
Flung it from his sling, to bring
That giant down.

I wonder if the stone
That struck Goliath's tome
Was also round and reddish brown?
Perhaps.... perhaps not.

You're the one I chose
Bright, round, red stone!
Reached down -- water to my elbows
I suppose....
Like an imprisoned son or daughter
Until rescued from that water
So I claimed you as my own
Tucked you in my vest
And headed home.

Oh sure, there were other rocks around you
In the water where I found you
Each one unique as well,
With histories of their own,
If they had voice to tell --
I left them to their watery grave
For some other chap to save.

Perhaps.... perhaps not

Nov 2015

Confessions of a Biker

Funny how - of a sudden, come
thoughts of childhood
Some pretty wonderful
Some not so good:
You could ride the streets or sidewalks in those
days
Share the road - key thing: stay safe
Brand new, bright red, J.C. Higgins
I guess I was not yet seven
On a sidewalk in Springfield, Oregon

She was wending her way up the hill
Arms full of groceries
Must have been in her 50's, 60's maybe 70's
Now I'd been many a time
on my brother's handlebars
But never solo'd on a bike before

So, I'm flying down that hill
Grocery bags all got spilled
I didn't stop - not even to say,
"I'm so sorry, Ma'am
From her lips came so much more than, "Damn!"

**I didn't have that brake pedal thing worked out
yet
And sure! It was an accident...
But it was so much more than that
When all is said and done
It was a terribly shameful hit and run....
On a sidewalk in Springfield, Oregon.**

December 2012

<u>Resolution</u>

And why should I, as many men I know,
Let others guide- lead their goal or gain?
Instead, I'll dig myself up from that hole
And choose my own along life's road to fame.

If like a tramp am I, in rags and tatters –
Or finely garbed in beautiful array,
My soul is still the same -- so little matters,
To squander what it holds would be the shame.

Eastward runs the wide Conformer's Highway,
The bypath for "Specifics" lies ahead;
On crossroads -- counting people going my way,
I see the countless hordes march East instead.

On worthy things I'll spend my time – be wise,
And list' to none but God, until I die.

A Sonnet:
Spring 1960

Should Have Gone To The Movies At Red Lake

I'm *not* going to see Jimmy Stewart
wearing glasses!   He's a cowboy!
Cowboys don't wear glasses!

"Suit yourself. Stay home!" dad said.

Decided to be a hero....
Plow the field. "Oh,
look!" they'll say....
"He plowed the field."
"How nice!"

Big, red Farm-All Tractor out of the barn.

Low on fuel
Siphoned some from
55 gallon drum

First swallow
Realized I didn't have the knack

Sweaty!
Chest pounding!
Almost heart attack!
Screaming!

Running deliriously around barnyard

Dizzy!
Drunk....
for...
For, for, for...
well....

Until I ran out of gas!

True story
Myron at age 9
Beltrami County, Minnesota

<u>Artificial Intelligence!</u>

Silly to think we're mere accident
Silly to think there's no plan
You marvel at roses and cry,
"How magnificent!"
Yet all you got is 'Big Bang.'

You hold the wife's hand at
The birth of your daughter
You count the babe's fingers and toes
You cradle her, say she looks just like her mother
Yet proclaim there's no Supreme Cause

Was your great, great, grandfather's
father an ape?
Perhaps his great granddad before him?
At which point in time did that
Ape gene-pool break,
And degenerate into human?

Talk about faith! Talk of religion!
You say it's a matter of science.
God laughs from the heavens,
And says to His Son,
"Look! Artificial Intelligence!"

Look all around at the spawn of today
The holes in the ear lobes and nose
The safety pins, lip rings, tattoos on display
I suppose they'll be one day ingrown!

Go back! Take another look at that rose!
Examine the petals, Smell the aroma!
The fool has said in his heart there's no God
You're not a fool, Buddy, are ya?

So before you go spouting the wisdom of men
without checking to see if it's false or it's true
Become a scholar! Use what you've been given!
A good place to start is Psalm 2.

Nov 2015

Home From Big Bear

Dad said, "You drive!"
    "Raymond!" Mom said
       "Don't you let the boy drive!"
But, down that mountain road we raced --
16 years old ... Confident! No problem...

Blue and white Oldsmobile Super 88, 1951.
Pushed along by that monstrous 22 foot trailer;
Aluminum, brakeless weighty four wheeler

Every twist and turn increased the pace
    Trailer and Olds had quite a race.
    Halfway down brakes are smokin'
We were prayin' but nothing spoken --

    Now it's serious; we were flyin
I'm yellin', "No brakes!" Mom's a cryin'
    "Stop signs comin' up--What do I do?"
"Lean on the horn, boy! Go on through!"

Now Artesia -- Route 91;
Flat land... rolled to a stop onto the gravel-
shoulder
16 years old ... Shaking! White knuckles...

Pop said, "Son, Guess I should take over."
Peeled fingers off wheel -- one by one...
That evening we pulled in our drive...
Wonder we got home alive --

Everything I told is fact--
Been there .... phew! --- done that.

recalling summer '59

DEFACTO *a.k.a.* *WASHINGTOWN*

One final, swiggy, swirly slurp --
The goblet dry, no further use --
Now pen comes forth, and I -
No longer shy -
Sit me down to scribble.

Been awhile, I mutter..
And in whose style?..I utter;
(to myself, of course ...).
I try to sit, but somewhat lie,
To limn some profound, worthless dribble.

Of love, and life,
And hope ...-Oh, CRIPE,
My blasted brain's a'spinnin';
Too many charged up, sparkin' wires
Attached within this furrowed mire
of greying cells,

(Now there's a fleeting thought, I think...)
.... But how to note with perfect ink
Is well beyond my penning.
I only think I think this thought:
That, rather perfectly, I am sot.....
With tasty fermament:
Some red, some white, some clear... or not,
(I don't remember);

Now a drinking fella's thoughts are clear,
Some say - with cheer,
And I confess, I must concur, For,
somewhere in a state ofblur I
met a chap – in fact, all three: A
Sage, a Mage, a See...

ahhhhh,
I've now forgotten - blindsided by that last
comment,
Let me just go back to pages past -
...Oh! yeah...
The Gove'ment!....

Our flag flew -- her valiant years --
In teaching solid ethic;
But common folk don't know the half...
For mind you, predators abound ...
They've always circled Washingtown...
Looking for the fatted calf,

Nibble here,... ah, tender bite,
Cunning, veiled in cloak of night...
Andrew Jackson held them at bay.....
But, Alas!...Jackson's ilk have gone away --
In runs the FED, the IRS, Tri-Lateral Commission
The World Bank, IMF-- beat the good folk to
Submission

Run around like they was gods!
Nothin' but a pack'o frauds!
DEFACTO ! sir, DEFACTO!

U.N. walks in, sets up shop --
No way folks can make them stop
I see I'm still a little sot!
But........on I plot.... er, plod!

Where's Sam Adams when we need 'im?
Folks is cryin' out fer freedom!

Oooops!
Now, where was I ? oh, my!....
how could I forget?
I ain't dead yet!

So skulking coyotes, snakes and less - abound...
Have made their lair in Washingtown!
Now before I finish up my rhetoric
Soberly, and not in jest..to say it kind: Pathetic!

Today, In Washingtown where freedom stood,
Should stand a bust of Ridinghood!
And at her shoulder -- shy, demure, aloof,
Should lean a smiling, well-fed wolf!

M. F. After an evening
clearing out
the liquor cabinet   2005

<u>*Sweatin' Bullets*</u> ...

or
April 15

Sweatin' Bullets to the wire

Something everyone should hire
Record keeping wasn't high --
(Now, that's one fact I'll not deny)
on list of things that I aspire to,
Lots of things I'd rather do
than taxes.

Every form completely filled
Every drop of blood be spilled
Do not alter, twist or spin it
Make doubly sure your check is in it;
Don't staple, mutilate or bend
Do not forget today's the day to send
Your taxes.

Lots of things I'd Rather Be Doing

They slink like hitmen for the Mob
Smirk and say it's just a job
These black suits--Just who are they anyway?
Were they born in my community?
Slimy filth! With impunity ...
I Wonder -- Do they claim immunity
from taxes?

April 15, 2004

Book Seven

Took A Turn For The West

The Professor

Prof. Wescan - Head School Master-
He could cipher with the best;
You start a poem or name a book,
And he'd recite the rest.

His hands were manicured, but gnarly,
And he walked a little bent;
Genteel, comely, manly air --
Everywhere he went.

To see "Sire" Wescan with his cane --
Bespectacled, hoary hair --
The ladies swooned,
Old men said 'Sir',
Still *very* debonair...

And the parents?
Truly grateful, just knowing he was there.

§ § § §

Now the Circle T was the biggest spread
'Cross th' Kansas line,

And Ramrod Lee gave a decent fee
To the extras he could find.

For these hired 'drifts' are needed sore,
At roundup'n brandin' time.

An' they bring their "reputations" with 'em
Always, when they come;
Ya gotch'er bright, yur slow,
Yur good, yur foul,
Yur mean, yur bad, yur dumb...
An' Lee could mark a talent, quick,
And weed out most th' scum.

Now, Reg'lars hit the spread 'bout May --
an' stayed 'til season's end,
There was me an' Shorty, Lefty, Mitch,
There was Slim an' Bow-Laig Ben.

Now, Bow-Laig had the 'rep' of bein' the
"Best to ever hit the 'T' ",
Hell, ropin', ridin', bustin' broncs -
He's twyst as good as me.
He could cut a calf from 30',
Brand 'er, an' rope another --
By the time the first could stagger up,
'N run, 'bawlin', to her mother.

An' broncs? Huh!
They knew that they'd been rode
When Ben was up-a-straddle;
13 years I'd seen him rode;
13 years an' ne'er been throwed....
Ears back, buckin'
Foamy sides --
Kickin' Snortin',
Terrified ! --
Then tremble,
'Xausted -- from the ride --
Ben'ed jus' pat their neck,
Toss reins aside....
.And step down from the saddle.

Only ever once did I see - 'most 7 year ago,
A pony cantered in the ring
To give ol' Ben a go.
This nag was special frisky,
And gave 'im quite a ride;
She hit the air five ways at onest
And broke his ribs - inside.

Ben, he swore 'You S.O.B.!
"You just had yer chance!"
He tore his spurs into her flanks --
But she just picked up the dance.

She raked his laig along the rails
And crunched him on a post,

Us boys had seen some rides before,
But never by a ghost!
His face was white,
his jaws was tight,
His eyes was steely grey,
But he'd never given in before,
And he wouldn't start today.

So, 20 minutes more they fought,
An' of a sudden, she was done.
Ben stroked the mare, and yelled at Lee,
"By damn! She almost won!"

He dropped to kiss the corral floor,
Then sat there in the dust - 'n
Jerked a rope, tight,round his laig,
Still laughin' an' a cussin'.

We picked him up, (he couldn't move),
All shoutin', "Yore the winner!"
"But you'll need Doc..."
"Hell no! Been working! Hard!
Think I earned some dinner!"

Doc set the bones --
"Yore broke up, Son!
Give that leg a chance!"
"She's got three days til payday,Doc,
Then we're heading for *The Branch!*

Cuz every month we'd get our pay,
an' go skeedaddlin',
Whoopin', hollerin'
To *The Branch.*
Ah, *the Branch*!
Its lure of poker chips and gin;
Its smoky, crowded, noisy din!
Its touch of soft flesh on rough skin!
Its "Hello, Shorty. Where you bin?"
Its comfortable, 'perfumee' Sin...
Its laughter- music- d ance.

Ahhhhh yes!
The Branch!

But, drink? -- And cuss?
That man knowed words ...
Could shock the entire Navy.
Hootch in Ben?.... to stop the pain???
Why, he went downright crazy!
Drunk and lame,
He went overboard;
Tossed "Joe Piano"
Out the door,

Sat on the stool and pounded keys, Why,
he massacred "Sweet Laura Lee", Then,
bowed hisself down to his knees -- An'
passed out
On the floor.

To see that cowpoke layin' there -
"He's better'n that! It don't seem fair!"

"Lefty's right." Little Shorty said,
"He should be mendin', home in bed".

Well, Ben was like a 2-ton bag....
We had to tie him to his nag...
Took Lefty, Shorty, Mitch an' me,
Then we mounted-up, -
An' home to th' "T"'.

So,
"Bow-Laig" We all call 'im now.
An' you know when,
An' you know how.

§ § §§

On a porch near the town of Sharon Springs,
Across the Kansas line,
Sits a long-retired Professor,
Just sipping summer wine;
He dwells on eager faces....
His children - taught to rule;
And he wonders: what their place is?
When they left his humble school.

Did any of them master life
and rise to their potential?
Or did they simply join the strife
of getting old and wrinkled?

And then he thinks of summers spent,
The Mays through mid-Septembers --
Of Britain, Spai n, the Continent --
Then of things he best remembers:

The screen door opens,
Breaks his stride --
"It's chilly, Sir. Please come inside."
He drains the glass
And nods his head,
"In just a minute, Sam", he said...

Then, back in time,
stares at the glass
"That mare! --
She nearly kicked my ass!"

For a moment he's just thirty three --
But the night air brings reality.
Wistful smile, picks up his cane,
He's Professor Wescott once again.
Shuffles through the back porch screen...
And, quietly, it closes.

Summer 2002

The Incident at Ol' Norm's Lineshack

Driving rain, comin' down
Northeast wind was fierce
Drummer pulled his collar 'round
Looked upward and cursed.

"We'll never make Red Rock tonight
An' I think we're in fer snow;
That wind has got some fearsome bite,
An' still 30 mile to go."

"Yeah, up ahead, about a mile,
Is that ol' lineshack a'Norm's;
Let's hunker down in there awhile -
Weather out this storm."

Witherspoon was trailing blood
Face was full'a pain
Don't know how he rode so good -
"Damn this icy rain!"

"Witherspoon can't ride much more,
And horses tuckered out --"
"Lineshack sounds purty good fer shore"
I answered, "Ain't no doubt."

We pushed the horses through the trees
At a slow but steady pace;
The muddy ground had begun to freeze
By the time we reached Norm's place.

From the darkness up ahead
There came a horse's whinny.
"Didn't count on that!" I said.
"Let's go see how many."

"You boys go on ahead, ya hear? -
I think this here's my time."
"Witherspoon, stop actin' queer.
This ain't no time fer dyin.

If them horses up ahead
Is who we think might be,
Pure luck we find 'em here," I said --
"And, Especially", croaked Witherspoon,
"The bastard that kilt me...."

§ § § §

Now, Norm had a makeshift stable,
A few bales of hay and stalls
Wired up to the shack by cables...
Didn't have no walls.

Drummer and I dismounted,
Threw our saddles in a pile;
Seven horses Drummer counted
Gave an ironic smile...

"This night could get real int'restin',
Might just earn our pay."
But I wasn't really listening,
I was spreading out some hay.

"Come on down from off that nag!
Lay down, Jeb Witherspoon.
I'll go grab my Remedy Bag
Have you fixed up real soon."

Drummer tugged an' pushed Jeb's leg
Easy o'r the saddle,
Then, sliding down from off his nag
I caught him -- Twas a battle.

Soaking wet with rain, blood, sweat,
The old Ranger shivered slightly.
"I guess yore right, I ain't dead yet,
But I couldn't do this nightly."

We laughed, I gave Jeb's arm a squeeze
And a big mouthful of rye.
Drummer mused, "Why don't booze freeze?"
An, we all guessed as to why.

As usual, Witherspoon answered best:
"Ain't got time" is all he said.

My kit was full of gauze and stuff
That mostly doctors carried;

I'd used it afore on a few good men -
Some I'd later buried.

I knew I had some matches there
     Wrapped up in a pouch.
"We have to cauterize that hole
     Once we get the bullet out;

Plus, we need some light to see
     For us to do this dance."
Drummer, he agreed with me-
     We had to take that chance.

"You take care of that old man
     You git yourself some light
Dig that slug out if you can
     I'll stand watch all night."

So I ripped the shirt from off his chest,
Saw the hole through his left shoulder;
I swore. "Half inch closer to his breast
     He wouldn't get no older."

Gave Witherspoon another jolt of rye
     And dug in with my blade,
The old man tried hard not to cry
     But he turned a whitish shade.

I poured more rye into the guy --
     Both his shoulder and his lips;
Held up the slug to show him why --
     Grabbed it with his fingertips.

Just as the blade went in the fire
     And turned a flaming red,

Drummer mumbled, "Company, Squire!"
"Shit!, Can't stop now!" I said.

"Do your thing, and I'll do mine,;
There's two so far, I guess

I'll take care of them just fine,
But the shots will bring the rest."

So I laid my blade on the open wound --
How it sizzled in that shoulder!
And a piercing cry left Witherspoon
While Drummer raised his smoothbore.

The ponies, mine and the other nine,
Had been munchin' hay all night;
But the shotgun echoing through the pines
Put an end to quiet.

Witherspoon lay fast asleep -
passed out from shock, more like, 'n
Rest of the night he didn't make a peep
Though round 'im was terrible fightin.

Ponies in their hobbles,
Completely terror-stricken...
Went all round that blood stained hovel,
But Old Jeb didn't waken.

§ § § §

Daylight saw an end to rain
and the ponies were well-rested,
Headed for Red Rock again,
This time more invested.

For, slumped in every saddle
And fair roped down with sisal
Was victim to a battle
The object of reprisal

§ § § §

And Witherspoon?
Useless as tits on a boar!
During the fight, 'n all through the night
All he did was snore.
I thought the horses would trample his ass for
shore

We left him back at Norm's to heal
Before trekkin' into town --
With lots of time to shape his spiel
Before he comes on down

--He'll twist his mustache - (as he does) -
Flash his star as he strolls 'round town
Tell everyone how bad it was
Tip his hat to folks around --

Yeah, his version will be stretched a bit,
And it will certainly have mass appeal
But, Drummer 'n me? Hell, we'll swear to it.
After all... he's just bein' Witherspoon ---
Ain't no big deal !

May 9 2015

The Big Elk River Incident

My name was John
Was a preacher's son--
    Could say, I was gentle-born
But talk of nuggets
Big as buckets
Lured me round the horn.

I teamed up with Jim --
Now, when I first eye-balled him
Th' fella seemed a good-enough sort;
Course, from what I know now
Just can't see how
My eyesight was so dadgum short.

Started pannin' fer yeller
On the Big Elk River
And come up with nuggets and dust;
Jim? His luck was fine
But nothin' like mine --
I saw he was no one to trust.

Queer breed, Jim -
It just oozed outta him...
All that greed and jealousy;
Sure, he used a pick
And you might say t'was quick
But it took several hours to kill me.

My brain grew dull
When he cracked my skull
With no, not one ounce of remorse;
My spirit, though,
It watched me go,
And vowed that ol' Jim would get worse.

There's more to be told
If I may be so bold
And a lesson or two might just reach yer,
So just take a minute,
Sit back while I spin it...
Recall, I'm son of a preacher.

§ § § §

"Well, Piss!
I'm done with this!
I've had all I can stand!
I'm headin' back
O'er that mountain, Jack"
The young miner then flung his pan.

"Oh, hell's bells, Mort!
Sure we've come up some short -
But we're partners, my young feller!
Sure, four months it's been;
But don't you give in!
Somethin tells me
We'll still see some yeller."

The old miner ran
And reached for the pan
Where it hid in between two large stones.
But his hand stopped short -
And he hollered, "Mort!
Come here an' look at these bones!"

The bones were white;
Dry and bright -
Maybe a year -- maybe older;
Parts of a shirt
Still caked with dirt
Fluttered from, could-be, a shoulder.

"Where's his kit -
And his other shit ? -
An, where in hell's his rifle?"

"Got a bashed-in head
That's why he's dead!
Been messed up - more'n a trifle!"

"Looks like a pick
Did the dastardly trick
It's laying o'er here on the ground;
prob'ly left him fer dead
With it stuck in his head --
Ain't no other truck can be found.

Them bones has been chewed
By some critters fer food
An' it looks like one whole leg is missin'"
Mort's mind overworked:
"Don't spose this poor jerk
Was roasted and 'et by th' assasin?"

Jack grimmaced at that
And then he shot back
"Hell no! He's a cowardly sort;
He prob'ly just saddled
Up and skeedadled...
So stop all those wild visions, Mort!"

Mort shook his head,
Coughed, sighed and said,
"Can't leave him like this, Jack. Can you?"
"Naw, Just as you say.....
I'll go, get my spade -
It's the Christian 'an right thing to do."

So they dug a big pit
put my dry bones in it
Took 'em, I guess, four-five hours --
An' I must admit
Those boys they had grit
With that one little spade of theirs.

These two boys, these -
Really, gents if you please,
Showed respect like some fellas that care.
From my foot to my tome
They laid out each bone,
And when finished, Jack offered a prayer.

By the time they were done
The daylight was gone
So, beside me, the two spent the night;
What a surprise!
When they opened their eyes!
And they saw what they saw at first light.

There, in the dirt
That was so hard to work
Was nuggets, some big as your fist!

Yes, under that tree
Where they dug and laid me
Was bonanza that they woulda missed.

§ § § §

And of Jim?
What became of him?
Low-down piece of slime --
Wasn't just
My skull he crushed;
Stole that mule of mine.

Now my Maggie Jean
She thought she was queen
Would have no bully master --
Jim used a goad --
Aw, he shoulda knowed
Cuz then, behold - disaster!

Jim Shouldn't Have Used A Goad

Short and sweet
With both hind feet
Just above the liver
I heard ol' Jim shriek
All 600 feet
Then I saw him float down Big Elk River

Ya' know I felt it comin' --
That weasely vermin...
So under that tree went my kit;
But young Mort an' Old Jack
They got it all back,
Uncovered e'en more than I'd hid.

Now, that there's my story --
Like I said, a mite gory,
But I swear on my grave that it's true.
Yep, I'd convinced Jack:
Never quit; don't go back!
'Twas the Christian 'an right thing to do."

- April 2015

Dead Wolf-Dog Mine

Down from the mountain came the old,
grizzled miner,   with a loaded down
Pack mule an' three wolf-dogs behind'er
Headed o'er to the assayer's shack
flipped open his saddlebag, pulled out a sack

Wolf-dogs just sat there as did the mule
Snarled, snapped and brayed at one or two fools
After ten minutes the old miner appeared
Whooping it up - the whole townfolk heard

The five crossed the boulevard to the hotel
Bought a round for the house - the whole
clientele -
Cost him a buck for a shave and a bath
New suit of clothes cost a buck and a half
Spent two or three more on a cute Calico
Another round for the house'n back out he did go.

Wolf-dogs snarled when he reached for his mule
Cried out in shock, they still came on, cruel
Attack was so sudden, ferocious, complete.
Tore him apart right there on the street
Nothing to do but to shoot'em -- all three.

Nobody knew whereabouts of the ore,
(If the assayer knew he ain't tellin' for shore).
So, his Glory Hole they never could find...
To this day it's still called
The Dead Wolf-Dog Mine.

November 2015

Miracle on the Red

The trail we'd traveled had been tough,
But we're almost done for shore --
1880, only April 24.
We were raw and tired and sore,
But we'd been this way before,

Lacking a day we'd been two months out –
Now, just ahead, reckoned Tim, our scout
Lay a lady trail herds talk about,
She'll sometimes scream, she'll sometimes
pout
A fearsome, boiling waterspout --
That can turn your insides, inside out:
The Red!

So, while Bill the cook doused the coals,
Herd spread out upon the knolls,
Boys and I rehearsed our roles –
An' heat lightning played o'erhead --

'Now The herd should hit Doan's Crossin'
A bit before midday,
And we know what lays 'head of us,
An' we'll surely earn our pay;

We've had some tough ones in our time,
But this is one to dread ---
The Mighty Red --
With fifteen hundred head."

I smiled across at young Jim Frank
As we stepped up in the saddle.
How I loved this kid, I thought,
As he sat there -- proud -- astraddle.

The other ten were lusty men,
But honest, upright, bright;
Roping steers or riding herd
Or e'en the rare gunfight
With rustlers, Pawnee, all left dead --
But now – we faced the Red.

With Buck and Skeeter ridin' swing,
The Miller boys on flank
I set the pace for ol'Doan's place
And sang out, "Move 'em, Frank!"

Cows, well rested from the night,
Seemed agreeable all right,
Agreeable and well-fed;

Oh, sure, a few decided to head back down,
But my two drag cowboys turned 'em round,
And my wrangler chased a couple down;
"So far, so
good".. I said
"Now let's cross that Red"

§ § § §

My first glimpse of the River
Gave me goose bumps up and down;

She was high and swift and full of foam --
Lived up to
her reknown!
But other drives had come this way -
They made it ...
Or they drowned...

Doan's Crossing on the Red River
Is no more 'n just a shack ...
Ol' Doan had a cable tied each side
To pull a wagon forth and back.
Hanging from the cable
And swinging fore and aft
Was what Ol'Doan called a ferry,
To me twas just a raft.

I slowed the drivers to a halt
To graze cattle on the hill
While I rode down to meet Doan hisself,
And I took Frank and Bill

When we walked into Ol' Doan's place,
Shudda seen the look on Ol' Doan's face!
Disbelief ! I remember it, still --

"I see your herd on that there hill,"
He looked at me, then Frank, then Bill --
"You can't cross at her swift pace.
Gotta wait! Least 20-30 days!
You'll lose least half your head!
She's the Red!"

"Take a ride along her banks,
Count the many markers;
See where men have tried and died
At the mercy of her waters!

Come, pore through copies of my notes
I've written home to most the folks --
The wives, the sons, the daughters;
Oh, I tell you, son, don't try this one -
She'll take your steers, your horses, guns
And spit you out like fodder!"

Your boys thirsty? Bring'em down,
Ol' Doan'll buy the first two rounds.
Your cattle ain't goin' anywhere,
Grazing land is more 'n to spare --

Much too early for other herds
To try to test the Lady.
Hell, other men besides your ten
Ain't nearly half as crazy!

So grudgingly, I asked young Frank
To ride up and get the others;
Miller boys stayed behind to watch;
Besides they said they'd ruther.

I explained real careful and complete
What ol' man Doan had said,
We took a vote, 8 to 1...
Gave in to Lady Red

About that time, a Miller kid
Came roaring down to Doan's;
Said fire was raging cross the Red,
And smoke and flames was showin'.

We all scrambled up the hillside
To calm them bawlin' critters,
Sang some old time cowboy songs
Like 'Bury Me Not', and 'Git Along'
An' for shore before too awful long
They stopped their skittish jitters.

Now in this massive evening glow
The river put on quite a show --
She ran blood red all through the night
As far as eye could see;

At the time it seemed so strange I know,
But that Big Red River seemed to slow

As fire raged on the nor'east side,
Just eatin' up the trees.

Jimmy Frank shook me awake,
"You gotta come 'n see this, Jake"
"I been up the river bed -
3 feet deep is all," he said.

"Right! and I'm the Queen," I drolled;
But I pulled my boots on like I's told
The darkness covered up his smirk,
But I played along like some damned jerk

Rubbed my eyes at the sight I met –
Hard for me to believe it yet --

A damn, big log-jam further north
Had cut the river in some sort
And left us with a little creek,
In spots not more than ankle deep!

"Awake the boys! Let's move some cattle!
We've got 20 miles to travel!
No time for grub til we get across;
Let's show this Lady just who's boss.

Wake Ol'Doan and get the chuck".
Doan came, pullin' on his pants –
said, "What the f --- ! Whoa !....
Man ! What luck !"

"Yeah, Doan. Log jam further up"
"Doan, drop that ferry, Load the chuck!
Drag 'er o'er water, rock even muck!"

We worked as mad men racing Red --
"Keep moving, boys, or we'll be dead!"
Cowboys pushed cows, slow but steady;
Cowboys nervous, queasy, sweaty!

§ § § §

Three hours later we were done,
We lost no steers - not a single one;

**Did lose a wheel on Bill's chuck wagon,
Blamed him for "uncalled-for draggin."**

**Three days later
At the roundabout
we were paid in full
For the two months out.
I got \$320 – not that great --
But Hell, it was only April 28**

- July 2013

Book Eight

At Last ... Sunlight!

A Lovely Garden

I'd like to try, my dearest friend
To never ever make an end
Of telling you - to thus express,
(If my verse may stand the test)
Describing thoughts I've thought - it seems
For decades – (some erotic dreams)
Others of "what might have been"
Had things been different way back then.

Had I perhaps been more a man,
Had I a crystal, read a hand;
But you know what? Perhaps (just musing),
I may not have been your choosing!
Those fifty years God had His plan –
And you and I but players;
Now, delightfully, the time has come
To peel off fifty layers.

I think our past matures the mind,
Corrects a wrongful tread;
What's gone before is training ground
For that which lies ahead.
Can we erase time as we go?
Not His plan - I don't think so...
Love is a salve, a burden halved;
As together trumps a solo.

A Garden Is More Than Flowers...

It's Love!

I feel such a part of you,
All the pieces fit;
50 years you've been with me,
But only recent met.

Oh, I'll work beside you night and day,
Scatter seed, work the clay;
Some passersby will see us toil,
Maybe frown as we tend the soil.

But others may express delight
At Pinks, Stock, and Pansies bright,
Call out as they pass by our yard,
"Ummm, You have a lovely Garden!"

Spring 2013

Insatiable the Fire!

Flick'ring, warming, growing
Kindled, ever fanned by desire
Yearning
Drawn into the comforting sweetness that is you
Ah, insatiable the fire!

Flick'ring, crack'ling, aflame
Blazing as the tongues reach ever higher
Rapturous
Burning within the loving completeness that is
you
Ah, insatiable the fire!

Flick'ring, glowing,
Ever smouldering
Basking
Content midst hues of sunset-sereneness that is
you!
Ah, insatiable the fire!

October 2015

Beneath a Sheltering Willow Tree

Beneath a sheltering willow tree
At the edge of my newly-purchased farm
I stumbled upon what appeared to be
An encirclement of old wrought iron

Fastened together so carefully
Old bed posts from what I could see
The height of it was about three feet
Maybe ten feet wide and twelve feet long
Iron so rotten It was almost gone.

Some kind of pen I first supposed
But when I saw some age-old roses
Twining round that iron on either end
I decided then twas a garden
I envisioned some early settler's cabin,
With this willow tree in their front yard 'n
Thought how lovely it must have been

But further examination proved it to be
A long forgotten cemetery
Tall grasses almost hid the stones
Marking out the family bones.

A jumble of thoughts rushed through my head
What to do with these newfound dead

I made my mind up then and there...
God had put them in my care

Each stone became a precious cause
Be they saints or be they outlaws

I determined to be their groundskeeper
Determined to dig a fair bit deeper
Just who were they before the Reaper
Lay them in their tomb?

I got down on bended knee
And began to weed beneath that tree
Seven stones I could clearly see
Within that wrought iron room

The stones were all remarkable
Each marble plaque was carved with skill
Each one told a unique story
Father, Mother, two girls, three boys
Hard years of the family's history.

Cleared of weeds, I could finally read
The first, a tragedy, indeed:

Mary Martha McKinley Ericksen
Born May 5, 1807
Flood took her away from me
Along with little Jeremy
April 23, 1842
And he only three...
Way too soon.

As I toiled beneath that tree
I thought of scriptural prophecy

How bones would rise from out the mud
Join up with sinew, skin and blood
And I spoke aloud, as I pulled out weeds
To the seven waiting there beneath.

"Yes,
Mary Martha McKinley Ericksen
It was indeed
Way too soon....
But, Mary,
Along with Samuel, Reuben
Of course, your little Jeremy,
David, Martha, and Lillian,
There'll for sure be a resurrection."

I could see that entire family
Smiling up contentedly
Beneath that sheltering willow tree.

December 2015

My Love

My Love, you establish my heart
You reassure my every part ---
You enfold me, you hold me
Inside !
Your perfumes, your mouth - your taste lingers,
You cause me to blush with your fingers!
I sup on your mouth, breasts, your toes,
And I drool as I nibble on each one of those...
Together - inviting, exciting, delighting -
We ride !
My mind explodes with your every caress,
Spiritual, sensual - each stroke, honest.
Desire flashes boldly, we give openly -
Wide!
Exhaustion - You lie still - in my arms;
I count, meditate each of your charms
I feel your calm breath, warm on my chest
I thank God we give of ourselves: the very best
Rapture; Ecstasy; Bliss.
Ummmm, One more deep kiss...
Our home -- at rest,
now and forever --
Abide !

September 8, 2012

Flour Sacks

Sat in Grandpa's parlor
Going through his cherished,
Dog-eared rows of books
His bookcase: just two shelves
Covered by a curtain
Like the curtains that covered
Grandma's kitchen window,
In vibrant, cheerful hues of pink
And that hid the shelves of her pantry cupboards
And the ones beneath her kitchen sink

And just like the aprons, blouses and skirts
That Grandma wore....
All, carefully hand stitched
With frugality, humility
And of course, her skillful ability --
All from brightly patterned
Cotton flour sacks

Within the bright,
Floral wallpaper- covered walls
Furnished with their "best they could afford"
furniture --
Highlighted by
Two wooden rocking chairs
sitting side by side
Grandpa had hewn them with care and pride...

Now visible by kerosene lantern light:
Flanked by small tables on either side,
And in between one more -
covered in the same flour sacking --
could have been apple crates under;

I sat cross-legged
'neath a flour-sack covered window --
Looked across the room,
Mesmerized by shadowy, dancing silhouettes
In the flickering lantern-light
Ghosting their way
Through the hallway into the kitchen
Returning to me with phantom arms
Filled with the aromas of allspice and cinnamon.

Transfixed but for a moment, the spell now gone,
As the sun --
Pouring through the flour-sack curtains
Easily defeated the kerosene.

Warmth and love flooded over me ...
I looked down at the two books
I had brought from Grandpa's bookcase.
I chose *Kazan, Wolf Dog of the North.*
And, bordered by flour sacks,
I began to read.

Dec 2015

Successful Career

Successful Career - To love only you,
Excellent pay - fringe benefits, too...
Working with you -- such happy days!
24/7; No need for a raise...

Smile is enough for the things that I do
Your laughter -- more than compensates, too;
Love reflects in your eyes – the payment I need,
Your warmth -- your response! – A bonus indeed!

Lifetime commitment agreed and then made...
Partnership! Weekends and holidays paid,
Rewarding career for the rest of my life
A Joyful Career – You as my wife.

Myron Feb 2014

<u>*TIMELESS -*</u>

Morning rays reach out with gentle,
caressing fingers,
Hollow, shadowy places fill slowly
across garden;
Orange blossoms waft fragrance on fresh
morning   breeze ....
Bee sings, gathering nectar;
Gazanias yawn and stretch to meet the sun --

Butterfly flits from petal to petal, sipping dew;
Finch twitters from low branches,
Raven croaks delight, splashing in birdbath...

Harmony.

Door bell rings
Time stops
Door opens a peep
Smiles
Hands touch
Warmth, light,color
Love ...

§ § § §

Morning rays reach out with gentle, caressing
fingers,
Hollow, shadowy places fill slowly across
garden;
Orange blossoms waft fragrance on fresh
morning   breeze ....
Bee sings, gathering nectar;
Gazanias yawn and stretch to meet the sun --

Butterfly flits from petal to petal, sipping dew;
Finch twitters from low branches,
Raven croaks delight, splashing in birdbath...
Dog whines,
Prancing below scolding squirrel

Music plays...
Laughter,
Distant traffic noises -- drowned out by silent,
delicious contentment.
Our corner of the world -
All is at rest . . .

Timeless!

Myron Ferdig
December 2014

Fini

To order this, or other works by author, go to
www.ferdigwerks.com